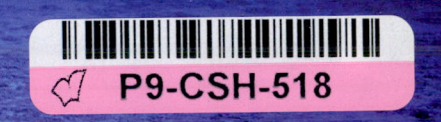

P9-CSH-518

Praise For

THE

DEEP

ONE OF NPR'S BEST BOOKS OF 2019

"A compelling story about the power and necessity of history and memory, community and connection. Do not miss this book."
—Ann Leckie, Hugo and Nebula Award–winning author of *Ancillary Justice*

"A striking book with original, fantastical worldbuilding. A harrowing survival story about transformation, and uncovering and reclaiming hidden history. Read it."
—Martha Wells, Hugo Award–winning author of The Murderbot Diaries

"A moving, dreamlike tale. Solomon's book (and clipping.'s song) feels like it's at the forefront of a new wave of speculative fiction unearthing the narratives of the historically silenced and lending them the voice of modern popular mythologies—sci-fi, fantasy, and everything in-between. It's thrilling to watch that wave crash to shore."
—Indrapramit Das, award-winning author of *The Devourers*

"A harrowing and impactful story of memory, duty, drowning, and the weight of history and what it means to very different people. I loved it."
—Aliette de Bodard, BSFA Award–winning author of
The House of Shattered Wings

"Solomon's beautiful novella weaves together a moving and evocative narrative that imagines a future created from the scars of the past. Highly recommended for those interested in SF or fantasy that draws upon the legacies of colonialism and racism to imagine different, exciting types of futures."
—*Booklist*, starred review

"With shades of Hans Christian Andersen, Ursula K. Le Guin, and Lois Lowry, plus inimitable explorations of difficult social interrelationships, Solomon's short tome is, indeed, a deep read."
—*IndieBound*

"Solomon packs a lot into a slender package, giving new voice to the story of people borne out of the horrors of the Middle Passage . . . *The Deep* is about the impossible weight of memory, a burden that must be shared to be borne. It is beautiful and terrible and vital, a story that comes from the very depths of our rough history, transforming as it surfaces and then returns. What was thrown down can rise up."
—BarnesandNoble.com

"Afrofuturism with a folklore twist . . . *The Deep*'s slim page count disguises the depth of the work within. Rivers Solomon conjures a vast world in their latest novella, one where history and present day collide and love can change lives. The text is ever-changing as the ocean itself. Shifting from third person to first person plural, at times it feels as lyrical as the song from whence it came. The story unbalances and redefines. It will trail in your wake long after you finish it. Yetu is a force to behold, and I for one am immensely grateful that Solomon allowed us to witness her story."

—Tor.com

"Gripping and profound . . . Pacey yet incisive, fun yet intelligent, gutting yet conclusively uplifting, Rivers Solomon has crafted a delightfully rich diet-confection in literary form. Let it wash over you—when you get to its optimistic end, you won't feel like drowning."

—*FIYAH*

THE
DEEP

THE
DEEP

by RIVERS SOLOMON

with Daveed Diggs, William Hutson,
and Jonathan Snipes

SAGA PRESS

LONDON SYDNEY **NEW YORK** TORONTO NEW DELHI

SAGA PRESS

AN IMPRINT OF SIMON & SCHUSTER, INC.

1230 AVENUE OF THE AMERICAS, NEW YORK, NEW YORK 10020

Copyright © 2019 by Daveed Diggs, William Hutson, and Jonathan Snipes

Afterword copyright © 2019 by Daveed Diggs, William Hutson, and Jonathan Snipes

Jacket art copyright © 2019 by Micah Epstein

First Saga Press trade paperback edition August 2020

SAGA PRESS and colophon are trademarks of Simon & Schuster, Inc.

For information about special discounts for bulk purchases, please contact Simon & Schuster Special Sales at 1-866-506-1949 or business@simonandschuster.com.

The Simon & Schuster Speakers Bureau can bring authors to your live event. For more information or to book an event, contact the Simon & Schuster Speakers Bureau at 1-866-248-3049 or visit our website at www.simonspeakers.com.

Jacket design by Sonia Chaghatzbanian

Interior design by Vikki Sheatsley

The text for this book was set in Sabon LT.

Manufactured in the United States of America

10

Library of Congress Cataloging-in-Publication Data is available.

ISBN 978-1-5344-3986-3

ISBN 978-1-5344-3987-0 (pbk)

ISBN 978-1-5344-3988-7 (ebook)

To the ornery and ill-tempered

—R. S.

This book and the song
for which it's named would
not exist without the work
of Gerald Donald
and James Stinson.

—clipping.

THE
DEEP

1

"IT WAS LIKE DREAMING," SAID YETU, THROAT RAW.
She'd been weeping for days, lost in a remembering of
one of the first wajinru.

"Then wake up," Amaba said, "and wake up now.
What kind of dream makes someone lurk in shark-dense
waters, leaking blood like a fool? If I had not come for
you, if I had not found you in time . . ." Amaba shook her
head, black water sloshing over her face. "Do you wish
for death? Is that why you do this? You are grown now.
Have *been* grown. You must put those childish whims
behind you." Amaba waved her front fins forcefully as
she lectured her daughter, the movements troubling the
otherwise placid water.

"I do not wish for death," said Yetu, resolute despite
the quiet of her worn voice.

"Then what? What else would make you do something so foolish?" Amaba asked, her fins a bevy of movement.

Yetu strained to feel Amaba's words over the chorus of ripples, her skin drawn away from the delicate waves of speech and toward the short, powerful pulses brought on by her amaba's gesticulations.

"Answer me!" Amaba said, her tone desperate and screeching.

Most of the time, Yetu kept her senses dulled. As a child, she'd learned to shut out what she could of the world, lest it overwhelm her into fits. But now she had to open herself back up, to make her body a wound again so Amaba's words would ring against her skin more clearly.

Yetu closed her eyes and honed in on the vibrations of the deep, purposefully resensitizing her scaled skin to the onslaught of the circus that is the sea. It was a matter of reconnecting her brain to her body and lowering the shields she'd put in place in her mind to protect herself. As she focused, the world came in. The water grew colder, the pressure more intense, the salt denser. She could parse each granule. Individual crystals of the flaky white mineral scraped against her.

Even though Yetu always kept herself tense against the ocean's intrusions, they found their way in; but with her senses freshly unreined, the rush of feeling was dizzying. This was nothing like the faraway throbbing she'd grown used to when she threw all her energy into repelling the world outside. The push and pull of nearby currents upended her. The flutter of a school of fangfish reverberated deep in her chest. How did other wajinru manage this all the time?

"Where did you go just now? Are you dreaming yet again?" asked Amaba, sounding more defeated than angry. Her voice cracked into splintered waves, rough against Yetu's skin.

"I am here, Amaba. I promise," said Yetu quietly, exhaustedly, though she wasn't sure that was true. Adrift in a memory that wasn't hers, she hadn't been present when she'd brought herself to the sharks to be feasted upon. How could she be sure she was here now?

Yetu needed to recover her composure. She'd never done something that dangerous before. She had lost more control of her abilities than she'd realized. The rememberings were always drawing her backward into the ancestors' memories—that was what they were supposed to do—but not at the expense of her life.

"Come to me," said Amaba, several paces away. Too weak to argue, Yetu offered no protest. She resigned herself for now to do her amaba's biddings. "You need medicine, child. And food. When did you last eat?"

Yetu didn't remember, but as she took a moment to zero in on the emptiness in her stomach, she was surprised to find the pain of it was a vortex she could easily get lost in. She moved her body, examined its contours. She'd been withering away, and now there was little left of her but the base amounts of outer fat she needed to keep warm in the ocean's deepest waters.

As evidenced by her encounter with the sharks, Yetu's

condition was worsening. With each passing year, she was less and less able to distinguish rememberings from the present.

"Eat these. They will help your throat heal," said Amaba, drawing her daughter into her embrace. Yetu floated in the dense, black brine, her amaba's fins a lasso about her torso. "Come, now. I said eat." Amaba pressed venom leaves into Yetu's mouth, humming a made-up lullaby as she did. Water waves from her voice stroked Yetu's scales, and though Yetu usually avoided such stimulation, she was pleased to have a tether to the waking world as her connection to it grew more and more precarious. She needed frequent reminders she was more than a vessel for the ancestors' memories. She wouldn't let herself disappear. "Keep chewing. That's good. Very good. Now swallow."

Spurred by the promise of pain relief as much as by her amaba's prodding, Yetu gagged the medicine down. Venom leaves slithered like slime down her throat and into her belly, and with every swallow she coughed.

"See? Isn't that nice? Can you feel it working in you yet?"

Cradled in her amaba's front fins, Yetu looked but a pup. It was fitting. In this moment, she was as reliant on Amaba's care as she had been in infancy. She'd grown from colicky pup into mercurial adolescent into tempestuous adult, still sometimes in need of her amaba's deep nurturing.

Given her sensitivity, no one should have been surprised

that the rememberings affected Yetu more deeply than previous historians, but then everything surprised wajinru. Their memories faded after weeks or months—if not through wajinru biological predisposition for forgetfulness, then through sheer force of will. Those cursed with more intact long-term recollection learned how to forget, how to throw themselves into the moment. Only the historian was allowed to remember.

After several moments, the venom leaves took effect, and the pain in Yetu's hoarse throat numbed. Other aches soothed too. The stiffness all but disappeared from her neck. Overworked muscles relaxed. Sedated, she could think more clearly now.

"Amaba," Yetu said. She was calmer and in a state to better explain what had happened that morning: why she'd gone to the sharks, why she'd put herself in such danger, why she'd threatened the wajinru legacy so selfishly.

If Yetu died doing something reckless and the wajinru were not able to recover her body, the next historian would not be able to harvest the ancestors' rememberings from Yetu's mind. Bits of the History could be salvaged from the shark's body, assuming they found it, but it was an incredible risk, and no doubt whole sections would be lost.

Worse, the wajinru didn't know who was to succeed Yetu. They may not have had the memories to understand the importance of this fully, but they had an inkling. It had been plain to all for many years that Yetu was a creature on the precipice, and without a successor in place, they'd be lost. They'd have to improvise.

Previous historians had spent their days roaming the ocean to collect the memories of the living wajinru before they were forgotten. Such a task ensured that the historian understood who was best suited to take on the role after their own death came. In addition to reaching into the minds of wajinru to log the events of the era, historians learned whose minds were electro-sensitive enough to host the rememberings in the future, and shared that information often and repeatedly with other wajinru.

Yetu never did this. The ocean overwhelmed her even when she was in its most quiet portions, and that was before taking on the rememberings. Now that she was the historian, it was even worse, her mind unable to process it all. She couldn't fathom spending her days traveling across the sea only to burden herself with more memories at the end of each journey. Unfortunately for Yetu, when the previous historian had chosen her, he'd been so impressed by the sensitivity of her electroreceptors that he'd failed to notice her finicky temperament. Yetu loved Basha's memories, loved living inside of his bravery, his tumult. But if ever he'd made a mistake, it was choosing Yetu as historian. She couldn't fulfill her most basic of duties. How disappointed he would be in the girl he'd chosen. She'd grown up to be so fragile.

"I'm sorry," said Yetu. "There's so much to tell you, yet I never know where to begin. But I am ready now. I can speak. I can tell you why I did what I did, and it has nothing to do with wanting to die."

Yetu readied herself to reveal all, to go back to

those painful moments and relive them yet again for her amaba's benefit.

"Shhh," said Amaba, using the sticky webbing at the end of her left front fin to cover Yetu's mouth. "It is in the past. It is already forgotten. What matters is that you are here now, and we can focus on the present. It is time for you to give the Remembrance."

The Remembrance—had it really been a year since the last? A year, then, since she'd seen her amaba? It was impossible to keep precise track of the passing of time in the dark of the deep, but she could ascertain the time of year based on currents, animal movement, and mating seasons. None of that mattered, however, if Yetu wasn't present enough to pay attention to them. The remember-ings carried her mind away from the ocean to the past. These days, she was more there than here. This wasn't a new thought, but she'd never felt it this strongly before. Yetu was becoming an ancestor herself. Like them, she was dead, or very near it.

"I didn't know that we were already so close to the Remembrance," said Yetu, unsure she even had the strength to conduct the ceremony.

"Yetu, it is overdue by an entire mating cycle," said Amaba.

Was Yetu really three months late to the most impor-tant event in the wajinru's life? Had she failed her duty so tremendously? "Is everyone all right?" asked Yetu.

"Alive, yes, but not well, not well at all," said Amaba.

A historian's role was to carry the memories so other wajinru wouldn't have to. Then, when the time came, she'd share them freely until they got their fill of knowing.

Late as Yetu was, the wajinru must be starving for it, consumed with desire for the past that made and defined them. Living without detailed, long-term memories allowed for spontaneity and lack of regret, but after a certain amount of time had passed, they needed more. That was why once a year, Yetu gave them the rememberings, even if only for a few days. It was enough that their bodies retained a sense memory of the past, which could sustain them through the year until the next Remembrance.

"We grow anxious and restless without you, my child. One can only go for so long without asking who am I? Where do I come from? What does all this mean? What is being? What came before me, and what might come after? Without answers, there is only a hole, a hole where a history should be that takes the shape of an endless longing. We are cavities. You don't know what it's like, blessed with the rememberings as you are," said Amaba.

Yetu *did* know what it was like. After all, wasn't *cavity* just another word for *vessel*? Her own self had been scooped out when she was a child of fourteen years to make room for ancestors, leaving her empty and wandering and ravenous.

"I'll be taking you to the sacred waters soon. The people will want to offer their thanks and prayers to you. You should be happy, no? You like the Remembrance. It is good for you," Amaba said.

Yetu disagreed. The Remembrance took more than it gave. It required she remember and relive the wajinru's entire history all at once. Not just that, she had to put order and meaning to the events, so that the others could understand. She had to help them open their minds so they could relive the past too.

It was a painful process. The reward at the end, that the rememberings left Yetu briefly while the rest of the wajinru absorbed them, was small. If she could skip it, she would, but she couldn't. That was something her younger, more immature self would've done. She'd been appointed to this role according to her people's traditions, and she balked at the level of self-centeredness it would require to abandon six hundred years of wajinru culture and custom to accommodate her own desires.

"Are you strong enough to swim to the sacred waters without help?" Amaba asked Yetu.

She wasn't, but she'd make the journey unaided anyway. She didn't want her amaba carrying her any more than she already had. The memory of Amaba's fins squeezing around her tail fin, dragging her away from the sharks at nauseating speeds, lingered unpleasantly, the same way all memories did.

She understood why wajinru wanted nothing to do with them but for one time a year.

2

IT WAS NO LONGER SUNG.

For that morsel of mercy, Yetu gave thanks. She understood why all the historians before Basha performed the
Remembrance to melody, that impulse to salvage a speck
of beauty from tragedy with a dirge, but Yetu wanted
people to remember how she remembered. With screams.
She had no wish to transform trauma to performance, to
parade what she'd come to think of as her own tragedies
for entertainment.

Wajinru milled the sacred waters, a mass of bodies
warming the deep. Yetu felt them embracing, swimming,
sliding against one another in greeting, all of it sending
a tide of ripples Yetu's way. The ocean pulsated. The
water moved, animated. The meaning behind their name,
wajinru, chorus of the deep, was clear.

Many wajinru lived far apart, alone or with friends

or mates in dens of twenty or twenty-five people. The wajinru had settled the whole of the deep but were sparsely populated. While there was the occasional larger group who lived together, up to fifty or one hundred, there was nothing like the cities Yetu had seen in her rememberings.

For a people with little memory, wajinru knew one another despite the year-long absence. They didn't remember in pictures nor did they recall exact events, but they knew things in their bodies, bits of the past absorbed into them and transformed into instincts. Wajinru knew the faces of lovers they'd once taken, the trajectory of their own lives. They knew that they were wajinru.

Because they tended to live so far apart, when they did gather en masse, it was an occasion of great celebration. Everyone shouted their greetings, swam in excited circles, joined together to dance a spiral. Soon, what had started as something intimate between two or three spread to twenty, then suddenly a hundred, five hundred, then all five thousand or six thousand of them. They moved spontaneously but in unison, a single entity.

It was this same energy Yetu would use to share the History with them.

"I'm relieved you're here," said Nnenyo, Yetu's care-maid during the Remembrance. When Yetu required everyone to hush, he would tell everyone to hush. When she needed stillness, he'd make everyone be still. If words didn't work, he'd compel them softly with his mind: a little nudge that felt to most like a mild, compulsive urge. A cough. A sneeze.

Few had such power of suggestion, but he was getting on, almost a hundred and fifty years old. The average wajinru lifespan was closer to one hundred, and while it wasn't impossible to live for so long, Nnenyo was the oldest wajinru in a long time. He'd learned to harness the electrical energy present in all wajinru minds. That was why he'd been elected to oversee the historians. He was the one Yetu was to inform about the next historian when she discovered who might be capable of taking on the task, and he was the one who'd facilitate the harvesting of memories from Yetu to her successor when the time came. If he was unable, one of his many children would take on the task.

"I'm sorry for the delay. I—"

"Bygones. You are here now. That is what matters. I have a surprise for you," Nnenyo said.

"I don't like surprises," said Yetu. She found it difficult enough managing the quotidian and routine.

"I know," he said. "But I couldn't help it. I'm an old man. Allow me my whims."

Yetu let his words wash over her fully despite herself. The warmth of his tone settling even if the raw sensation of it stung.

Nnenyo was decent. Though he preferred a life in the moment, free of the past, like other wajinru, he recalled more than average. Were it not for his age, he would've been the historian to replace the previous historian, Basha. Yetu was the next best choice.

"So? What is it, then? What's my surprise?" she asked quietly. She needed to save her strength and didn't want to waste energy projecting her voice.

Nnenyo had no trouble feeling Yetu's words despite the surrounding bustle of conversation. Yetu was focusing every bit of her energy on picking his words out of the onslaught of information pressing against her skin. "Ajeji, Uyeba, Kata, Nneti, now," he called with a sharp whistle that pierced through the water.

Yetu wanted to vomit the various food items Amaba had stuffed her with to strengthen her for the Remembrance. Her skin was an open sore, and Nnenyo's call had salted it.

"I apologize," said Nnenyo.

"Do not make such sharp sounds around her," said Amaba, who'd been working quietly near Yetu, minimizing movement in order to lessen the disturbance to Yetu. "Can't you see how it stings her?"

Amaba pampered Yetu now, but it hadn't always been like that between them. Yetu's early days as a historian were marked by endless discord with her amaba. It was only in adulthood that their relationship had settled. Thirty-four years old, Yetu'd matured enough to predict and therefore avoid most quarrels.

That didn't mean there wasn't still hurt. Unlike Amaba, Yetu remembered the past and remembered well. She had more than general impressions and faded pictures of pictures of pictures. Where Amaba recalled a vague "difficult relationship," Yetu still felt the violent emotions her amaba had provoked in her, knew the precise script of ill words exchanged between them.

"Such things don't matter with all of this going on," Yetu said, though it was a lie she told just so Nnenyo didn't feel bad. He was close enough to her that the impact had bombarded her full force.

Amaba looked on the verge of arguing, then seemed to think better of it, returning to her work instead. She was wrapping sections of Yetu's body with fish skins and seaweed to help block out sensation. It wasn't a perfect solution, but it would make the Remembrance more bearable.

Nnenyo's children arrived not long after. They'd been far away to conceal the surprise, so Yetu couldn't discern the shape of it. Of course, the gift was wrapped, but that didn't always matter. Sound traveled through everything, and though a second skin could dull things, it usually wasn't enough to hide something completely.

Ajeji, the youngest of Nnenyo's children at only fifteen, handed Yetu a corpse. Still reeling from the shock of Nnenyo's whistle, she accepted it without pause, question, or upset.

"Don't worry," said Ajeji. "We did not kill it. It was already dead. We just thought it'd make a good skin for your gift."

A vampire squid, strange and complex in form, did make a good disguise, though she hated holding it. She dealt with death every day during her rememberings, and more again when she was lucid enough to hunt for food. For once, she wanted to avoid confrontation with such things, reality though it may be. It never ceased to trouble her that peace depended on the violent seizing and squeezing out of other creatures.

It was perhaps dramatic to compare that to her own situation, but it was true. Her people's survival was reliant upon her suffering. It wasn't the intention. It was no one's wish. But it was her lot.

"Such a beautiful creature," Yetu said, front fins massaging the squid so she could memorize the shape of it. She had not yet determined what gift lay inside, too enamored by the textures of the externals. "I have never touched one or even been this close. Remarkable."

She wanted to cry for the dead thing draped in her front fins.

"You have always been such a tender thing," said Nnenyo as Yetu clutched the vampire squid. "Does it help to know that when we found it, there were no marks upon it? It did not die at the hand of another, as far as we can tell, but peacefully of age."

Yetu nodded. It did help. She didn't understand why everything couldn't be like that. Gentle and easy. No sacrifice. No pain.

Yetu handed the body back to Ajeji, unwilling to break inside the creature's flesh. "What's inside of it?" she asked.

One of Ajeji's siblings—Yetu guessed Kata by the precise, jagged movements—opened up the slit they'd cut in the flesh cut and removed a small, flat object, which she handed to Yetu.

"What is it?" she asked.

"We don't know, but we know how much you like to have old things you can actually hold. It was found here near the sacred waters, lodged inside the skull of a two-legged surface dweller, which itself was inside the belly of Anyeteket," Kata said.

"Anyeteket?" she asked. She hadn't thought of that shark in some time. Anyeteket had only died last year but had lurked in these waters since the first wajinru six hundred years ago. Her age and infamy had earned her a name, which was not an honor bestowed on most sea creatures.

It wasn't common for frilled sharks to be bound by such a limited area as she was, but she had two reasons to stay: One, she'd probably never forgotten the rain of bodies that descended here when two-legs had been cast into the sea so many centuries ago. Sharks didn't usually feast on surface dwellers, but easy meat was easy meat. Two, being sickly, she couldn't travel far to hunt. Wajinru supplemented her diet by bringing her grub.

Yetu was intrigued by the present being offered her. She guessed the two-legs skull inside of Anyeteket had been what had made her so ill all these years. There was a chance the head was one of the first mothers, the drownt, cast-off surface dwellers who gave birth to the early wajinru.

Yetu rubbed the flat object from the skull against the sensitive webbing of her fins to get a better sense of its precise shape. Sometimes, when she came across something she'd never seen before, she could reach her mind out to the History and find it: a tiny detail she'd missed in one of her rememberings.

At first feel, the object resembled a jaw, for there were tiny, tightly spaced teeth, dulled by time. Closer inspection revealed something purpose-made. It was too regular, its edges too smooth, for its origins to be animal. There were complex etchings in it. Teeth marks? Yetu enjoyed the feel of complex indentations against her skin.

"A tool of some kind?" Amaba asked, her voice tinged with desperation. She was anxious for knowledge, any sort of knowledge, keen to fill the various hollows she'd amassed over the past year. The Remembrance was late, and her lingering sense of who the wajinru were had started to wane.

Yetu closed her eyes as she felt a remembering tug her away from the present. Amaba, Nnenyo, and his children were reduced to a distant tingling, and the wajinru who were gathered in the sacred waters felt like a pleasing, beating thrum.

In the sacred waters, there was never color because there was never light. That was how Yetu knew the remembering had overcome her, because there was blurred color. Light from above the ocean's surface peeked through, painting the water a dark, grayish blue. It was bright enough to reveal a dead woman floating in front of her, with brown skin and two legs. There it was, something pressed into her short, coarse hair.

It was a comb, a tool used for styling hair. Yetu flowed

from remembering to remembering. She could only find three combs in her memory. The one in her fin didn't seem to be one of them, but its origin was clear. It had belonged to one of the foremothers.

Yetu stared at the face of the woman in her remembering, not yet bloated by death and sea, preserved by the iciness of the deep. She was heart-stilling and strange, her beauty magnetic. Yetu couldn't look away, not even when she felt someone shaking her.

"Yetu? Yetu!"

In the remembering, Yetu was not herself. She was possessed by an ancestor, living their story. Not-Yetu reached out for the comb in the sunken woman's hair and noted the smallness of her own fins, the webbing between the more stable cartilage finger limbs not yet developed. She was a young child. Old enough to be eating fish, shrimp, and so on premashed by someone bigger, but still young enough to need mostly whale milk to survive.

The little hand grabbed the comb, then Not-Yetu was jamming it into her mouth to stimulate and soothe her aching gums.

During such rememberings, Yetu's loneliness abated, overcome with the sanctity of being the vessel for another life—and in a moment like this, a child's life, a child who'd grown into an adult and then an elder, so many lifetimes ago. Yet here they were together, one.

"Yetu! Please!"

It ached to leave the foremother, the peacefulness of

being the child, the comb, but she had her own comb now. Nnenyo had chosen his gift for her wisely.

"I'm here. I'm awake," said Yetu, but her words came out a raspy, meaningless gurgle.

"The Remembrance isn't long from now," said Amaba. "You cannot be slipping away like that so often and for so long."

Yetu was going to ask how long she'd been out, but as her senses resettled and acclimated to the ocean, she could smell that everyone was eating now. Hours had passed. It was the evening meal.

The rememberings were most certainly increasing in intensity. Years of living with the memories of the dead had taken their toll, occupying as much of her mind and body as her own self did. Had she been alone, with no one prodding her to get back, she'd have stayed with the foremother and the child for days, perhaps weeks, lulled.

Yetu might like to stay in a remembering forever, but she couldn't. What would happen to her physical form, neglected in the deep? How long would it take her amaba to find her body? Would she ever? Without Yetu's body, they couldn't transfer the History, and without the History, the wajinru would perish.

"Yetu. Pay attention. Are you there?"

It took everything in that moment not to slip away again.

During the Remembrance, mind left body. Not long from now, the entirety of the wajinru people would be entranced by the History. They would move, but according to instinct and random pulses in their brains, indecipherable from a seizure.

They would be in no position to fend for themselves in that state, so they built a giant mud sphere in defense, its walls thick and impenetrable. They called it *the womb*, and it protected the ocean as much as it protected them. Wajinru were deeply attuned to electrical forces, and when their energy was unbridled, they could stir up the sea into rageful storms. It had happened before.

Typically, Yetu was the last to enter the womb. There'd be a processional, and then she'd swim in, finally resting at the center of the sphere.

They were still building. When all of them worked together, it took three days, with no sleep or rest. The meal Yetu had awakened to them eating would be their last. They had to fast before the Remembrance so as not to vomit when the ceremony was taking place and to ensure their minds and bodies were weakened by starvation. That made them more receptive to bending. A historian needed her people's minds malleable to impart the History.

For her part, Yetu feasted, her only companions Amaba and Nnenyo, who alternated shifts every few hours. Nnenyo was off now to gather more food for Yetu and to check on the progress of the mud womb.

Amaba waited silently nearby as Yetu ate. She was still trying to build her resources. Get her fat up. If she slipped away into her mind during the Remembrance, her people would suffer, experiencing the rememberings without her guidance or insight.

Worse, the Remembrance might subsume her. Reliving that much of the History at once—it might kill her in the state she was in. She couldn't shake the feeling that it already had, that it had been poisoning her for the two decades she'd been the historian.

"Stop fidgeting over there, Amaba. I can feel you," said Yetu. "Why are you so anxious?"

"There hasn't been a day without anxiousness since you took on the History," Amaba said.

"It is different now. More. Tell me, what troubles you? Is it me? Come closer so we might speak proper," Yetu said, surprised by her own request. Closer meant she'd feel the ripples of Amaba speaking more forcefully, but it had been so long since they'd properly talked. She wanted to know what was on Amaba's mind and tell her what was on her own. She wanted to be like other amaba-child pairs, with a relationship unstrained by the duty the rememberings brought. It was never to be, but they could share a moment, at least.

"You have enough troubles of your own. You have the troubles of our whole people. I won't bother you with it. Now quiet. Focus on food and rest. The womb will be ready before you know it, and when it's done, you need to be here. Here, Yetu. You hear me? Here."

Yetu focused on the comb still clutched in her fin. She would ask that it be sewn up inside her in death. It was one of the few tangible things she'd touched of the past, a reminder that the History was not an imagining, not just stored electrical pulses. They were people who'd lived. Who'd breathed and wept and loved and lost.

"You are enamored with that thing," said Amaba, gesturing to the comb, her curiosity plain. Yetu hadn't let go of it since Nnenyo gifted it to her two days ago.

"It is special."

"Your remembering told you what it was, then?" Amaba asked.

Yetu stared out at the working wajinru ahead of her. They were a half mile away, and Yetu could just make out the rumblings of their actions pulsating through the water.

"Yetu? Are you here?" Amaba asked.

"I'm here."

The condemnatory shake of Amaba's head pressed familiarly across Yetu's scales, the burn dulled by its predictability.

"I don't like it when you suddenly stop answering. It scares me," said her amaba.

"You mean annoys you," Yetu said. "Not everything is about the rememberings, Amaba. I'm not a child. Sometimes it takes me a moment to gather my thoughts. Or sometimes I just have no desire to honor your questions with a response."

Yetu felt taken by the same indignation that had often overwhelmed her as a child, inflamed by the slightest of slights. Yetu appreciated Amaba's caring nature, but sometimes her gentle chiding turned into chafing, and Yetu was reminded of all that was wrong between them. Yetu would never be the easy child, nor Amaba the mother to give space. What hopes Yetu had for a connection beyond caretaker and caretaken were squashed. Would she always be just the historian, over time supplanted by the voices of the past?

Yetu shook her head, calming herself down. Amaba was just worried. She had every right to be. It had only been two days since she'd rescued Yetu from sharks. The specificity of the memory may well already be fading for her, but the feel of it, the fear—that stayed.

Amaba whistled softly. Had she been feeling less sensitive to Yetu's needs, she'd have screeched. Such a thing might've killed Yetu. That was the truth. "Why wouldn't you want to answer my question? It is a simple one, no?" asked Amaba. "Do you know what the object Nnenyo and his children gave you is, or don't you?"

"I know what it is," Yetu said, her head beginning to tense and throb. She'd had more interaction in the last few days than she'd had in the past year. Her patience was waning. She could only be the good daughter, the compliant wajinru, and the dutiful historian in short bursts. After a time, the constant conversation and stimulation wore her patience down. She was becoming a sharp edge.

"Well? What is it, then?" asked Amaba, letting her voice get away from her. She spoke loudly enough that Yetu had to swim away several feet. "I'm sorry. Though this would be much less difficult if you answered when I spoke to you, like someone normal."

"Someone normal wouldn't be able to tell you that the object is a comb. Someone normal wouldn't be able to tell you that a comb was a tool the wajinru foremothers used in their hair," said Yetu. "Someone normal would never know these things. Someone normal couldn't fill your hole. You are someone normal, and you don't know anything."

For several seconds, Yetu's amaba didn't speak. She had the look of something wounded, her fins moving in an agitated fluster but her wide mouth puckered shut.

Yetu should've felt guilty, perhaps, for her harsh and bitter words, but instead she soaked up the silence, drunk it like the freshest whale milk.

She didn't mean to be so cruel, but what else was she to do with the violence inside of her? Better to tear into Amaba than herself, when there was already so little left of her—and what *was* there was fractured.

"I'm sorry," said Yetu.

"No need. It is already in the past." Amaba swam closer, so the two were near enough to touch. "I demand too much. Ask too much of you. I don't even understand why I care so much about that stupid, what did you call it? Comu?"

"Comb," said Yetu.

In one of the rememberings, there was still hair caught in a comb belonging to the foremother. Salt water had washed any hair strands from the tines of Yetu's new comb, and now she could only imagine how the bonds of black keratin had once choked the carved ivory.

24

Yetu didn't explain to her amaba further. She would not be mined for memories yet.

This one knowledge, this one piece of history, it was hers and no one else's.

Nnenyo came back not long later with more food for Yetu, but she'd finally had her fill. Her stomach was bloated and overstuffed, so even though she was hungry, she could not bear to eat another bite.

She had become so ragged, not just since the last Remembrance but over the course of her youth and young adulthood. It all had a cumulative effect, didn't it? She imagined a sunken ship, heavy with cargo, pieces peeling and rusting away year by year like dead scales. Yetu wasn't as hardy as those feats of two-legs innovation, though. She would die, and corpses were not eternal.

"We are almost ready for you to join us in the womb," said Nnenyo.

"Already? So fast?" asked Amaba.

"They are ready for the History. They're working faster than usual, like nothing I've ever seen before."

So much for three days. It had only been two. Yetu wasn't ready.

"It will be fine," her amaba said.

Her stomach twisted and coiled, and her heart raced. She tried to settle herself, to feel the lovely, cool water entering her gills, restoring oxygen to her blood. But she was suddenly short of breath.

"Don't worry, Nnenyo. Like always, she will pull herself together in time," said Amaba.

In the early years, in fact, Yetu had been much worse, unable to keep down food or do such basic things as hold her bowels for more than a few minutes.

"How are you feeling?" Nnenyo asked.

Yetu nodded her head. "I will do what is asked of me."

"You are a blessing," said Nnenyo.

"I am what is required," she said, no warmth left in her even for Nnenyo. Everything tense, she just wanted this whole thing to be over. Fine. Let the Remembrance begin right here, right now, for all she cared, womb or no womb.

"Breathe," said Amaba. "Breathe."

"It hurts," Yetu said, ashamed of the vulnerability. She wanted to flee and be in her discomfort alone, like she'd been this past year. In front of Amaba and Nnenyo, it wasn't so bad, but the whole of the wajinru people would see her in this state. "I'd hoped to be stronger by this point," she said. She wanted there to be more of her, to be steady on her feet, or else the Remembrance would steal what remained of her.

"They don't care if you are strong. Only that you remember," said Amaba. "Do you remember?"

A flurry of tiny bubbles left Yetu's mouth as she sighed. "I do."

"Good," said Amaba. "That is all we ask."

3

WAJINRU FLAPPED THEIR TAIL FINS AGAINST THE water on Yetu's command, a steady, pulsating thrum in meter with her beating heart. The pitch of it was deep, so deep. Yetu let the massive waves of their movement consume her. She submerged herself in their energy. All her nerves left her, now that the Remembrance was beginning. The History was her power, and it ignited her. She could do this. She would do this. She would be their savior.

"Remember," Yetu ordered, voice filling the womb.

Yetu gave them a script, but they knew the words. It lived in their cartilage and their organs, as coded into them as the shape of the webbed appendages on their front fins or the bulbousness of their eyes. She only need remind them. That was all remembering was. Prodding them lest they try to move on from things that should not be moved on from. Forgetting was not the same as healing.

"Our mothers were pregnant two-legs thrown overboard while crossing the ocean on slave ships. We were born breathing water as we did in the womb. We built our home on the seafloor, unaware of the two-legged surface dwellers," she said. In general, Yetu didn't tell the Remembrance. She made her people experience it as it happened in the minds of various wajinru who lived it. At the start, however, she preferred to give them some guidance. It made the transition of memories much more efficient when they had context—context Yetu had never had. She'd discovered the History on her own, through out-of-order scraps and pieces. Slivers slicing through her.

Yetu twisted and tensed as pain overwhelmed her. That was something she should be over by now, after all this time, the physicality of it. But she felt her whole body go rigid and then snap. Her body was full of other bodies. Every wajinru who had ever lived possessed her in this moment. They gnashed, they clawed, desperate to speak. Yetu channeled their memories, sore and shaking as she brought them to the surface. The shock of it nearly knocked her unconscious. She had once imagined channeling as a sweet, beautiful flow of energy, the past running gently through her. It was more like slitting an opening in herself so they could get out.

Oh, was this pain real? It didn't even belong to her. Was there anything about her that wasn't a performance for others' gratification?

As Yetu's body moved with the pain, her subjects moved too. They didn't quite copy her. That would imply they could see anything but the black of the deep of the sea. They felt her and knew what to do. For once, all were in unison.

To see if the wajinru were ready to move on to the next stage, Yetu tuned in to individuals. Her amaba, Nnenyo, children she'd met over the years, her worshippers. Even with the rush of movement of their in-sync bodies, she could feel unique flourishes in each person. They each had a signature.

She couldn't determine which was worse: the pain of the ancestors or the pain of the living. Both fed off her. The Remembrance had officially begun, but she hadn't gotten to the actual *remembering* part. This was the preparation. Stretching their bodies so they could be open to the truth.

She was weak—couldn't handle the pain, and she wept to think about what was coming.

"Remember," Yetu said again, her voice quiet, sharp, deep, insistent, forcing them to know what she knew. "Remember how deep we go."

Their bodies became still but for the gentle flutter of fins to stay afloat, their scaled skin perked and ready to listen.

"Remember how deep we go."

As she said it, it became true.

She honed in on the bottom of the ocean, deeper than any wajinru of this generation had ever lived, the old homes of their ancestors destroyed.

She let her mind sink into the dark, dense, salty waters. So heavy. She pulled the wajinru down into the rememberings with her, as her mind reached out to theirs. They could not resist her magnetic energy.

They had to adjust to this new depth. Wajinru ruled the deep as one of the hardiest and most flexible of sea creatures. Their ability to survive in the dark, sparsely populated depths as well as hunt meat in the shallower, slightly sun-touched waters gave them an advantage. But the deepness that Yetu shared with them now was something different altogether. It was so, so low to the ocean floor. Though their bodies were protected by the safety of the mud womb, in their minds they had become someone else, taken by the remembering Yetu foisted upon them.

At first, struggle and breathlessness. Then an uncomfortable stillness, like being wrapped in layers of kelp, too disoriented to break free. The waters suffocated them.

Yetu felt Amaba's body cease to struggle and go limp, then someone else's, then yet someone else's, until every wajinru sunk together to the bottom of the womb, mimicking the falling bodies of the first mothers, just as Yetu intended.

"Remember," she said.

This was their story. This was where they began. Drowning.

"Submit," Yetu whispered, talking to herself as much as to them. She was begging herself to do what needed doing, what she told her mother she would do. As she commanded them to remember, she wished she herself didn't have to. The rememberings had stolen Yetu away. Who might she have been had she not spent the better part of her life in the minds of others?

Yetu sank into the pain, allowing her body to relax despite the intensity of feeling. She would transmit the story to them, as she had always done every year since she was fourteen, as historians before her had done for many years.

"Tell us!" someone shouted, their voice high-pitched, loud, and demanding, a screech that sliced through the water. "Tell us! Tell us now!"

"Remember," Yetu told them. "Remember."

It wasn't a story that could be told, only recalled.

The wajinru who'd shouted nodded their head, and soon every other wajinru was nodding as well. A dance of bopping heads, causing a beautiful pattern of zigzags in the water. It went from a nod to a dance, their bodies rising from the wombfloor where they'd sunk. They moved their shoulders, then torsos, then waved their fins.

"Tell us! Tell us! We must know!" the screeching wajinru called again. "I do not remember. I must remember."

"What is your name?" Yetu asked. The wajinru felt her soft voice easily through the moving water, so attuned her people were to her in that moment.

"I have no name. I am nothing. I am sunk!"

"Remember your name," said Yetu.

"No name! I have no name," they said again. "Help! Tell me!"

They were drowning in that deepest deep Yetu had

31

shared with them. Swallowed by the blackness of the below. "Remember!" Yetu said. "Remember now or perish. Without your history, you are empty." Yetu told them. "Everyone, shout this person's name so they remember!"

"Ayel!"

"Ayel!"

The chorus shouted their name. They were all in this together. They couldn't let any one wajinru get lost in the grief of the remembering.

Yetu joined the chorus in calling Ayel back into the fold.

"The feeling of emptiness will pass. Soon you will be overfilled," said Yetu.

Ayel swam up to her, weaving through the mass of wajinru. "I am starving. I am no one."

This happened sometimes. The process of remembering demanded an openness, and in some people, openness became nothingness. The void of the ocean washed out their identity as the History tried to get in. "Help me!"

Though it hurt to do it, Yetu reached out her front fins and grabbed Ayel's. She shared with the woman the image Yetu often used to retether herself: the first infant wajinru being rescued by a whale.

Images of connection. "Do you remember?" Yetu asked. "Do you remember this moment?"

Ayel said, "Yes, yes. I remember. I remember now."

Yetu transmitted the memory to the others as well, something to calm them.

Perhaps she shouldn't have started with the lonely

heaviness of the deep, not at a time when she was so consumed with her own loneliness. It was too much for them.

She couldn't help but feel sorry for Ayel and any others who were overwhelmed. They didn't know how to live with this pain. Yetu had become accustomed to it, its sharpness blunted by time.

"I'm here! I'm alive!" said Ayel, surprised by her own existence.

Yetu sent her back to the other wajinru and carried on. Pressure built up inside her as she called the History to the forefront. She and her people were lost in a bubble of agony. It went on and on.

There was no way to measure the passing of time, or whether time was passing at all. But traditionally the first part, where Yetu handed over the memories, lasted for hours, and the next part, where the wajinru soaked up all the memories, days. And though not all of it was suffering—there were times of true happiness, joy, whole decades of bounty—the sad moments were totalizing. So, arrested by the images, they were paralyzed. Through Yetu's machinations, the wajinru experienced the rememberings like they were living out their own memories. They were the ancestors.

Piece by piece, Yetu showed them their past, filled them with it. Soon, she'd give them all of it. It would be theirs, and she would be free from it, for a little while.

For a short time, the History would be outside of her. It was their people's one concession to the historian: three days of emptiness while they processed the rememberings.

Yetu rushed it as much as such a thing could be rushed. The people would not get the release they needed if she skimped. And any piece she left untold, she would keep. But she didn't want to keep any of it. She wanted to live how she had lived before she turned fourteen, before the History replaced Yetu with all the wajinru who had proceeded her.

"Hold on, hold on, hold on," she whispered under her breath, startling the wajinru. They swarmed around her, connected to her every thought.

"Yes, hold on," they said, feeling her struggle.

"Please, please," she said. She had to hold on a bit longer, then she'd get some peace . . . for a bit. Then another year wasting away as she neglected her own self for the History. Maybe she would finally die. Maybe that was for the best.

Yetu remembered, remembered, and remembered. She called to the memories, drew them to her, then pushed them out to her people one by one in an unrelenting torrent. Not quite sequentially, but a complete telling of their story, with some sections rearranged as necessary.

She remembered the first mothers, the images of their floating bodies as seen by their children or other wajinru. She remembered whales, their gigantic, godlike forms. She remembered shelters made of seaweed and carcasses. Castles, too, made out of the bones of giant sharks. Kings and queens. Endless beauty, endless dark. Then death, so many deaths. Looming extinction. The History of the wajinru included triumph and defeat, togetherness and solitude.

As always, the unfolding of the rememberings was influenced by Yetu's own recent experiences. She couldn't let go of what had happened a few days ago with the sharks. She couldn't distance herself from it now. She couldn't forget as easily as her amaba did that she'd been so close to being eaten.

"Listen!" called Yetu to the wajinru. "Listen and remember, I command you," she said, her voice growing louder with rage and sadness, with every wild emotion she could no longer contain. This was her chance to let it explode out of her, and she would luxuriate in the combustion. They would feel pain, but she would feel release.

"Listen and remember, I command you," she repeated, then showed them the remembering that had possessed her a few days prior. It was the first remembering she'd ever had, and soon it would be their remembering too.

"Let it overtake you," she shouted, strained voice piercing the water.

They gave themselves over to it, copying Yetu's ecstatic movements. She shook her head back and forth so fast and so hard that she lost her sense of equilibrium as the remembering overwhelmed them. They all watched together in the remembering as hundreds of sharks gathered to share a feast of bodies that looked so much like them, just like wajinru.

"They're killing us!" someone screamed.

Shrieks and sobs erupted throughout the womb as they saw their brethren, sistren, and siblings gobbled alive by massive white sharks. "Wait!" someone called. In the remembering, they swam closer to the site of the slaughter, putting themselves in danger of becoming victims of the massacre. "Wait! Look! It's not us. It's not us!"

Closer up, the differences between wajinru and the strange floating bodies became clearer. Their tail fins were split into two. Two legs. They had no scales. They were land dwellers. Dead land dwellers at the mercy of the cruel sea.

Outside the remembering, wajinru knew what two-legs were. They knew to avoid them, to stay clear of shallow waters where their boats sometimes roamed. But in the remembering, it was like they were seeing them for the first time, possessed by the wajinru ancestor who'd seen this two-legs mass grave.

Yetu stopped speaking, stopped guiding the memories. It was a communal experience, and the wajinru needed to do some of the figuring out.

"The split-fins are our kin!" someone said.

Another said, "They are nearly our twins."

Their differences were great too, but anyone looking at the two creatures could see they were of the same heritage.

"I've never seen anything in the deep that looks so much like us," said another.

The moment the wajinru understood how related they were to the two-legs, the remembering changed, just how it had for Yetu two days ago. They were all now one of the floating dead bodies. Their lives recently extinguished, some spark still remained, brains starved for oxygen but pressing on. The wajinru felt the deadness like it was their own.

Like Yetu, they couldn't take it. It was too strange to carry both truths at once: the aliveness of their own bodies, and the deadness of the two-legs corpses. The conflict split their minds in half, threatened their own bodies.

That was why Yetu had squeezed a dragonfish to death, pried open its dead jaw, pressed its teeth into her scales until she stained the water red, then swum to where sharks hunt easy prey. To join the realities. To make sense of it all. Sometimes, the rememberings took precedent over everything else, even over the survival of the present.

Yetu saved them from wanting to die, pulling them out of the remembering when they were on the verge of breaking out of the womb to go to the sharks the same way she had. They still had far to go. There were still so many stories to tell.

It went on and on till she butted up against the memories of the last historian. For this, she had to brace herself. Basha, brave Basha. So much braver than Yetu, he had suffered more in his lifetime than she ever would. He had never let the rememberings steal so much of his power and strength. He had let them ignite him. She wanted it to be like that for her, too.

Yetu worked to push the remainder of the rememberings out of her, putting distance between herself and the memories. It didn't work. The pang of his eventual death shot through her. She could feel it so fresh, could feel her fins around his face as she harvested memories from him, living his life as if it were her own. How it hurt her to see his story unfold, to end. If such a vibrant thing as he could die, Yetu would meet that end sooner rather than later.

Despite the waves of pain rocking her into a catatonic trance, she continued. Images, stories, songs, feelings, smells, hungers, longings, tears—memories—left her mind. She coughed them up like something burning in her lungs, hoarse and ugly, the violence of it shaking her whole body.

And the wajinru swallowed them.

If she could just get this sickness out of her once and for all, the sickness of remembering, she would survive. She wanted to survive. She didn't want to be the wajinru with a death wish, who swam with sharks as she bled because she could not tell past from present.

The wajinru reveled in knowing, desperate for the stories of their past. Soon, they were full on it.

Yetu let herself feel her body. The cold, heavy water. The brush of currents. Her mind was empty. Blessedly empty. Nothingness filled her in a rush of heat. There was no one there. No voices, no stories, no visions of deaths.

Blissed out, she floated limply until she could no longer ignore the pings of water coming from the other wajinru.

She felt them, though for a moment she forgot who they were. She forgot who she was altogether, let alone who she was to them. Small bits of it came back to her. Her name. Her life. Her amaba.

It wasn't a complete picture, but from the scattered fragments, she understood one important thing. The wajinru were her people, and for now they were held captive by the History, living the lives of the ancestors from beginning to end. At some point, collectively, when they'd learned and internalized all they could, they would give the History back to Yetu, their historian, who would keep it for them while they lived out their days in blissful ignorance.

Yetu didn't know much, but she knew she couldn't let that happen. Not this time. Not again. Or she would die. She looked down at her own body, trifling and small. A mere wisp of dead seaweed billowing in the dark.

There were the burns. Amaba never knew about those, about the year Yetu became so sensitive to touch that she swam to the bottom of the sea and pressed her scales against a lava vent to scorch away the nerves. Her brain could not hold the History and the present. She felt the wajinru as they moved in the shadow of the womb, a great hulking black mass surrounding her. These were her people, her extended kin, but they were also death itself. When they'd had their fill of the rememberings, they would come for her and pour it back into Yetu, a cracked vessel.

In time, she'd be subsumed. She'd never been this close to annihilation before. It had always pained her to take back the rememberings, her own mind blotted out in favor of those who'd lived before. Those times, though, Yetu had managed to keep an inch of herself. Now she wasn't sure even a speck would remain.

The ancestors pulled her deeper and deeper into the abyss of the past with each passing year. How long before she didn't awaken from their summons at all? How long before, in a confused state and painted in blood, she went to the waters of the great whites like she had done before Amaba had found her? That couldn't be what they wanted, for her to disappear. Yetu felt the wajinru swarming all around her. Yetu knew what they would do. First, seize her. Next, gut her mind. Last, fill her empty shell with ancestors and pretend they hadn't just murdered Yetu by forcing her to endure these memories endlessly for another year. The thought of it made her shake. This time, she wouldn't emerge from it. There would be no Yetu left for the next Remembrance. She'd be dead.

Yetu wouldn't let them do it.

The ancestors were needy but rarely cruel. Surely they would understand why she couldn't do this again. To let the wajinru put the rememberings back inside of her would be to commit suicide. To live, she must flee. With a last look to her wajinru kin, soaking up their beauteous dance in the mud womb, Yetu left. She swam, and she swam, and she swam, and she forgot, the rememberings becoming more distant with each upward meter gained. They didn't need her. They were stronger than her, always had been. Where Yetu was sensitive and high-strung, they were free-spirited and happy. The History would not undo them like it had undone her.

Yetu did not look back, but she felt them in her wake. They were trapped in the memories with no one in the wings to relieve them of the burden. They were in the Remembrance now, one with every wajinru who'd ever lived. She felt them churning the water, even though the womb was supposed to prevent that. She felt them remember. Yetu feared the world would feel it too.

4

How strange we would've looked to the first mothers: wild, screaming fish creatures, scaled and boneless. What would they have made of our zigzag bodies curling through the water in a spirally streak? Perhaps it is a blessing that because of their deaths they could never look upon us. They never once had to fret over the strangeness they'd wrought.

What does it mean to be born of the dead? What does it mean to begin?

First, gray, murky darkness. First, solitude. Each of us is the only one of our kind, for we are spread apart and know not of one another's existence.

We die in droves, foodless.

We live only by the graciousness of the second mothers, the giant water beasts we've years and years later come to call *skalu*, whales, who feed us, bond with us, and drag us down to the deepest depths where we are safer. Sperm whales, blue whales, whales that are now extinct, whales so rare there are only one or two of their kind.

We live among them, they our only kin, unbeknownst to any one of us that there are others who would come to call themselves the wajinru.

Until one day—

We are Zoti.

Babies of all kinds are always wanting more: more touch, more food, more answers, more kindness, more world, more sea, more newness, more knowledge. But none want more than us, a little fish-child whose whale pod dies of grief when its matriarch perishes from a harpoon.

Another fish-child might've died, but we are so hungry that we swim to shallow, unsafe depths where we know food is plentiful. Without the pod to coordinate hunts, and too small to catch anything big, we feast on trout. It is not enough. We are so big now. We go shallower, to where the light stabs our eyes, blinds us.

It is days until we see food large enough to satiate. Something floating—a sea lion? Out this far from shore?

Our pod never preferred to feast on carcasses, didn't like the rot, but sometimes it was necessary. Right now, for us, newly orphaned as we are, it is necessary.

We swim toward the floating creature, but it is not dead. It is not even sleeping.

It turns toward us, first with a look of shock, and then with a look of fear.

It is smaller than it should be. Emaciated. And it cannot swim well. Lashes on its back. It is a surface dweller of some kind. A land animal.

Despite our hungry belly, we cannot eat this creature, whose face is so captivating, drawing us in. Something familiar and warm circles through us, a memory written in our blood.

Though it looks like a stranger, we, a small and scaled squirming thing, had come from the belly of a being like this.

Is it a penguin or another animal who split its time between sea and land? Did we come from a pod of them who all died, making them virtually extinct? Was this thing here the last of its kind? How lonely. We must save it, or at least make sure its last moments are not spent alone.

It makes noises at us. Nonsense.

Its brown skin peels and flakes.

We grab it with our fins and it screams. Swimming on our backs, we move our fins quickly in search of land. The movement of the water means we're not too far from a small island.

The creature gurgles as water lands in its mouth, but this is the best thing we can do to keep it above water. We could go faster if we swam on our bellies, carrying it underneath, but with that length of a journey, a land dweller would die.

This surface-dwelling creature with split fins—two legs—is bigger than us, but near weightless in the water, and we finally are able to drag it to shore.

It makes noises again, all of them incomprehensible.

Every day we bring it lobster, shrimp, crab, or fish. It does not eat it how we eat it. It has put three large flat stones together over a little pit where it rubs sticks together until they spark orange like the inside of a glowing fish. Then it lays whatever we've caught for it that day over the flat stones until they sizzle white stuff and turn golden brown. The scent of it is divine.

We begin to understand the things this strange creature says, and the more we do, the more we begin to think of it as *her*. *Water* means where we live. *Land* is where she lives. *Sky* is what's above. *Sand, stone, trees, fire, hungry, hot, cold, sweat, sad.*

She talks and talks, and we listen, captivated by the noises. She is nothing like our pod, friendly and warm, but she gives to us in her own way. She gives us time. She gives us objects to explore. She gives us words.

Every day, we recognize more of them. *Bark. Spice. Cut. Bruise. Scale. Fin. Us. Tomorrow. Yesterday. Light. Dark.*

As we grow, we learn, until we can make sense of almost every noise that comes from the two-legs's mouth. The fascinating world of the surface dwellers opens up to us. Their technologies and creatures. Their ways of seeing. "You are perplexing," she says to us, and though we don't know what perplexing is at first, we begin to as she uses it to describe other things: mysterious tracks in the sand, a washed-up object she can't identify. *Perplexing* means a problem she hasn't solved.

She is always trying to understand the world. She is like us. Hungry for more. She is curious about how to make plants spring up from the ground, how to make the plants into nets she can use to catch fish.

Whatever she knows, she shares with us, and we soak up her every word. Not just facts. Not just the names of things. Stories.

When with our pod of *skalu*, we only hummed—long, low howls that filled the depths so we might find one another. It's difficult to achieve at first, but after a time, we try to copy the land creature's noises and make them our own.

We want to tell her things the way she tells us things. We want to share everything we know with her. We want to tell her that she's special. We want to tell her that we'd only been searching for food those months and months and months ago, but instead we'd found—we don't know the word for her yet. We will invent a new word. Our land creature is worth a new word.

After copying and copying her, we learn to make sounds with our throat and tongue. They do not sound like the surface dweller, but after a time, she understands. As she looks upon us, we can tell the land dweller still thinks us perplexing. She says she has always known there was a world beyond this world, a world where the unseen happens, but that we surprise her still.

We like that we surprise her because that sounds like it's a good thing. Warmth floods us.

"You did not come from a god," she says. We don't think she means this cruelly, but it bothers us still. We know a god is a special thing.

"Could you be our god?" we ask, words hoarse and croaky.

We would be content to spend our days basking in her presence, swimming in the water as she fished and told us stories.

"I am too small to be a god," she says.

Indeed, a year has passed and we are her size now.

"Why do gods have to be big?" we ask.

"I do not wish to talk about this anymore," she says.

The land dweller will no longer engage in conversation about where she came from or how she came to be floating half dead on driftwood in the middle of the sea. We wonder if her god abandoned her.

When the creature asks us where we came from, we say that we only remember a little. We remember a face like hers. Just like hers. We remember the ocean. We remember chewing the fleshy seaweed that bound us to our first mothers.

"How can you know all of that?" she asks.

We don't understand the question. We just remember. Every moment is a spark, and the spark is there forever.

We do not speak how she speaks, deep and smooth. Our voice is a raspy, clicky mess, and the two-legs often struggles to parse us.

But in the water, we make beautiful sounds with our

throat, and from the creature, we learn how to name the whole world, the whole sea, using this thing we only had a half idea of. Language.

Now we have a name for being alone. A name for being anxious. For searching. For fear. For denial. For ugliness. For beauty. For wanting something and someone.

"I am Waj," the two-legs says one day.

We are out in the ocean, she on the shallow, sandy ocean floor, and we just beyond it so we have more room to swim, our head above water. At first we think she means that's the name of what kind of creature she is. A waj. Soon, it is clear she means that it's a name just for her, to distinguish her from others.

"What does it mean?" we ask.

"Chorus or song," says Waj.

"What's a song?"

And then she sings for us and we are in love.

We do not have a name that can be spoken in the way Waj speaks, nor do we have a name at all. A unique pitch, perhaps, that our pod called us by, but that was a different sort of thing.

"Will you name me?" we ask.

Waj smiles and laughs. She reaches out to touch our cheek the way the whale did with its jowl when we were but a pup.

"I will call you Zoti Aleyu," she says.

We know those words together mean *strange fish*.

There is a gap between us that cannot be bridged. We live in the water, she on the sand. We sleep alone below the surface. She sleeps on the beach. She is tired, angry, and mad with loneliness. We are too.

She builds a raft from pieces of the island, and we ask her where she will go. "Back home," she says.

"Where is that?"

But she is done talking except to say, "Do not follow me, strange fish. Savior. We must each be where we belong."

"What is belonging?" we ask.

She says, "Where loneliness ends."

We do as she asks and do not follow, but when she is out of range of the distance we can feel, we immediately regret it. We swim as fast as we can in the direction she has gone, chasing any trace of either the feel of her paddles in the water or the smooth surge forward of her sails up and catching wind.

On the third day of searching and finding nothing, we feel a storm working itself into a vortex above us. A giant spiral of doom for anyone on the water or near a shore. We don't know if the land creature is caught in it, but we must save her if there's a chance she is. Neglecting food and rest, we look for her.

Our search is unending, and when the hurricane comes, sweeping the center of the ocean into mad, mixed-up sludge, our search for Waj becomes a search for wreckage. We never find even that.

The moment we first ever saw Waj all that time ago, a year or two years or maybe more, floating, looking like something good to eat, we could not have known what she'd come to mean to us. Perhaps it would've been better never to have understood, to have stayed in that moment full of possibility.

We've lost our pod. We've lost our two-legged surface dweller.

For days, we drift. We are not worried about dying, though we are not yet at the point where we are wishing for death. That time will come. Moons from now.

Waj had said she was returning to the place where she belonged, and that belonging meant not feeling lonely. We do not have a place to return to, as our pod is dead, and we are alone, the abandoned creature Waj had dubbed us Zoti Aleyu, a suitable name for something singular and alone, but perhaps—

We dive down to the deep where the second mother once dragged us. The pressure is immense and it squeezes us. We plunge through the cold, through the darkness. The deep will be our sibling, our parent, our relief from endless solitude.

Down here, we are wrapped up. Down here, we can pretend the dark is the black embrace of another. Down here, we eventually find more of us. A whale, one of the biggest we've ever seen, descends like a sunken ship. We tremble as it hums its song. *Waj.*

Its dive is right over us, and it swims closer and closer. Soon it will barrel right through us like a torrential wave, bowling us over, likely killing us. We accept this death. It is the very opposite of dying alone. We will perish much like we began, with the second mother heralding our passage between this world and the beyond world.

We don't close our eyes. It will be upon us in seconds. We are not afraid. We welcome it. This is belonging.

The whale, a few measures away, opens its mouth. Inside, there are pups, pups that look like miniature version of us. Little *zoti aleyu*. Strange fish.

We gasp. We are outside of our body. We wonder if the blue whale devoured us and we are dead, and this is the afterlife, a world of dreams.

The whale hums and our whole body shivers and shakes from the force of the vibrations. We don't understand its beautiful, hoarse moans beyond the most rudimentary levels of communications. It is kind. These little zoti aleyu are not gifts, and this whale did not come looking for us, but it recognizes that we are one kind.

"Welcome!" we say, gathering the pups, six in all, stretching our fins out to pull them into the fold of our body.

Having never been with child, we are without milk. How will we feed them?

"How will I feed them?" we ask the whale, a mix of shriek and song using mouth shapes not dissimilar to what the surface dweller used.

The whale hums. Again, we do not understand, but it stays with us. We're not sure how much longer it can lurk in the deep before needing to return to the surface to breathe.

"Where did you come from, zoti aleyu?" we ask the creatures so much like us.

We pull them close and nuzzle them. We watch their wobbly attempts to swim and move. Their scaled skin is softer than ours, and their faces are so tender, they're like the soft meat inside a clam.

They are different ages, some as many as two or three years. Some just born. The whale has collected them, has been taking care of them, and it plays with them even now. It won't abandon them. It will continue to give the milk we don't have to the youngest among them.

The pups mimic the sounds we make. When we say, "Hush now, sweet thing," they imitate approximations of the sounds all in unison. A chorus of "ooo"s and "eee"s and "eyeyeyeye." Their soft, whistling vocalizations are the most noise we've heard since our surface dweller left us. It is wondrous and overwhelming, and our skin is alive with the tingles of new waves and vibrations. Our ears are alert, ready to capture every new sound from these remarkable creatures.

We bring them close. We will not let them leave our side. Not like Waj did.

We do not cry, though we want to. We cannot ruin this happy moment with tears.

"There are so many of you," we say. "There are so many of me. Creatures just like me."

We ask the whale if there are more, and when it doesn't understand, we gesture to the little zoti aleyu and sweep our fins wide to suggest magnitude, volume, quantity.

The resulting moan of the whale is thunderous and sad. It cries. The pups giggle at the fluctuations in the water making them move and bounce, making their little pointed teeth chatter.

The cries carry on, and the pang of loss strikes us, too. There had been more at one point, perhaps. But now?

We mourn for every zoti aleyu, cast away into the ocean, eaten or starved. But we do not mourn long. If there are six right here, then there are more somewhere else. Or there will be more. We'll swim through every speck of ocean if we must to locate our animal siblings.

"I am Zoti," we tell our new pups. They are *our pups. Ours.* They will not know loneliness like we have known. They will have no true knowledge of the concept of abandonment.

In time, the pups fatten before our very eyes. Anutza, Ketya, Omwela, Erzi, Udu, and Tulo. Their names were words from the language the surface dweller taught us, and meant *together, many in one, never alone, family, connected,* and *kinship.* We are not ashamed that we put every hope and dream for them into what we call them.

To cover more territory, we ride the back of the blue whale to search the seas for more of our fellows. The pups squeal as we rush through the water. They make a lovely melody without even trying. Stuck so long with our own voice, we didn't know how good zoti aleyu could sound. Every sentence is a gorgeous song and their harmonies rip us in half because we are too full on contentment. Too happy.

First we find two. Twins. Not quite fresh out of the womb, but nearly. We look through the water trying to find where they have come from, but they have drifted too far.

We are nine in total now. Then we are sixteen. Then seventeen. Then thirty. It is only a few years later that we find some closer to my age. A pod of four. We cannot speak to one another, but their joy is plain. We are sixty now, then seventy. And yet we are one.

For those not from my fold, it is difficult to get along at first. They are without language almost completely, with but fifty or fewer concepts. They learn.

Ekren, when she learns to speak, sings a song to me and tells me to follow her. We do. Her purpose is clear. She wants to mate.

There are so few of our kind that—should we know how to do this? We don't.

Ekren does, and she shows us. Our bodies move in the water in an awkward rhythm until a passion takes hold and we are in ecstasy. After finishing, we swim back to the pod. There is possibility here, for more, to make more. There could be zoti aleyu who know who their parents are, whose past is not a question mark.

So we make more and more. We find more. We build. The deep is our home and we are filling it. This cold place will become a shelter for any stranded, abandoned thing. In this big wide sea, we are far from the only strange fish.

We become queen of this place. One of the eldest among us, we know what most others do not. For that, they call us historian.

. . .

To protect ourselves from those who'd destroy this precious thing we've fashioned out of scraps and leavings, we build cities. The materials of our structures are mud, carnage, ship wreckage, and plants harvested from more shallow seawater. Our language flourishes until we've lost count of the words. We have words for every creature in the ocean. We have words for every region of the water.

We hone our natural skills and learn how to hear one another across distances that span days of travel time.

And yet we, the maker of all this, want more and more and more. We are collectors, and a collection is never complete. This vast city of ours must endure forever, which means it needs more reinforcements. Thicker walls. More huts to home and protect the growing families. And more zoti aleyu. Our population, roughly three hundred, is still too small to be considered robust. We remember the way our centuries-old pod was wiped out like a flash. When not properly fortified, a legacy is no more enduring than a wisp of plankton. It is our duty to ensure that the zoti aleyu survive, and that means we return to searching the ocean for any who are stranded.

We are away now so often that children swim after us calling, "Zoti! Zoti! Stay! Stay with us! Tell us the story of the surface dweller on the brink of death you saved! Stay! Please!"

"I am making it so no one of us will ever be without a home again," we say, and shoo them off. We are in a hurry. We've planned for a several-week trip to the surface in hopes of learning the answer to our most pressing question: Where do the zoti aleyu come from?

One of the more precocious of the lot grabs us by our tail fin and pulls, then bites savagely. "Stay!" it says. "I despise you. If you go, I hope you never come back."

Its mouth is full of our flesh.

Injured now, we should have no choice but to obey the little zoti aleyu's request that we remain in the city we've made at the bottom of the ocean. We don't have time to nurse wounds, however. Every moment wasted is a moment toward our people's destruction.

Others come to gather the misbehaving pup, and we are off toward our lonely days of searching. It is a pleasant loneliness because in the end it will mean more togetherness. We are getting older and older, thinking more about what it is that makes a stable future when the world is so full of unpredictability.

Weeks are spent at the shallowest depths. Ships pass us by and at times we follow them, but to no end.

It's been almost half a year when we find another of our kind, a seven-year-old feral thing recently taken in by a pod of fin whales. It's blind and deaf, sensing only by its skin, which is heavily scarred and torn off in places. It recognizes, either by smell or feel, that we're like it, and swims up to us curiously.

We try to draw it to us so we can take it back to the deep before we continue our search for more zoti aleyu, but it will not leave the whales.

"Come!" we say.

It will not come.

We reach out our fins to grab it but the whales intervene. They are easily four times our size. Not to be trifled with.

We use our words so it might feel them against its worn skin, but the zoti aleyu is not having it. The whales hum in unison and we're stunned into paralysis by the vibrations of the sound waves. While we're immobile, the pod swims from us, the zoti included.

We have known too much loss. Right now, the whale pod is all that pup knows, but in time, it will want for more, and will it be able to find us?

It could find us if we were massive, if our dwellings stretched so high, their tips were in the shallow part of the sea. We need more workers. More builders. More zoti aleyu.

How disorienting it is to go most of your life wondering about a thing, only to happen upon the answer, and it is a horror.

We knew we shared kinship with the surface dwellers. For what else could explain our similarities, our ability to speak their language, our memory of the face so like Waj's during our infancy, floating still in the water?

But the full truth is not as we imagined it.

We lurk near the surfaces, hoping to find more zoti aleyu. We listen to the talk and chatter of two-legs on their massive ships. There are surface dwellers in the bottoms of these ships whose language we understand, whose words are the same ones Waj had used.

They are suffering and scared. They have been robbed from their homes, stolen from their families. Their lives are no longer their own. They belong to the two-legs on the decks of the ships.

We are descendants of the people not on the top of the ship, but on the bottom, thrown overboard, deemed too much a drain of resources to stay on the journey to their destination.

We know this because we see it. One day we are swimming but a few feet down from the surface in pleasantly cool waters, when there's a plop from above, a struggle causing the water to stir, and then a sinking.

The surface dweller is in our arms, heart still beating, but we are too far from any land for us to think of dragging it to an island. It is unconscious, and its belly is round with child. We bring it to the surface so it might breathe, but it never comes to. Underfed and malnourished, this is no surprise. We wonder how close it was to death already before whatever devil who captained that ship abandoned it to the seas.

The two-legs dies in our arms, but not moments later, its body starts moving, taken over by a spirit or some other thing of the next world.

Afraid, we let go. We don't wish to intervene with the dead. We watch from a distance, feel its convulsions in the water against our skin.

Its eyes are closed. It is dead, isn't it? Yet it moves as if something is inside of it, using its body as a vessel.

As we see the two-legs's belly move and bend, something

inside of it indenting the flesh, we understand its baby is trying to get born. The poor thing is trapped inside, and we want to help, but how? How can the body even push? We worry for the two-legs's pup and wonder if we should claw open the two-legs's belly. We can save the child in a way we couldn't save the parent.

We bring our teeth toward the belly of the dead, but we cannot bring ourselves to desecrate the flesh in this way. The fat round belly gives under our touch as we lay our cheek against it. We can hear the two-legs baby inside.

"Come out," we sing. "The world is ready for you, and you are ready for the world."

It's the birthing song we zoti aleyu sing for our little ones, and there's a chance that something in our voice will reach a two-legs pup too.

"My body is preparing milk for you," we sing. "You are hungry. Come to this world, so you might eat."

We look for the place where the baby is to come out. The *ashti*. The tunnel.

There's a round button on its belly that looks promising that we feel with our front fins, and we wonder if we have to nudge it to open. We press and press, but it does not yield. Then the surface dweller's legs begin to splay apart, and we come under it. We see it: the head. Our eyes widen, struck. It is not a two-legs head.

There are fins at the center of its back, on its sides, and at its front. Hairless. And darker than any land creature. It is zoti aleyu. It is zoti aleyu!

What magic had intervened to transform the pup in the womb? Was it the ocean itself, the progenitor of all life? Did the zoti aleyu have a god after all?

"Come!" we sing. "Come. We have been preparing for you. We have feasted so you will be strong."

The pup is coming. Head, shoulders. Then we grab hold and pull it out into our embrace. This close to the surface, we see its features so clear. Black eyes. Brown, nearly black skin. Beautiful dark scales.

We sing to it to rejoice, overtaken. We have never seen a zoti aleyu this new. This small. This fragile. How many who'd been just like this were swallowed whole? "Precious pup," we say.

We cannot think about its origins. We cannot think of what sickness plagues surface-life affairs that they throw living creatures to the sea to die alone. We must not think of the surface dwellers and two-legs at all. Only zoti aleyu.

"I will call you Aj," we say. It means small. This little thing in front of us is the tiniest of our kind in this moment. One day it will be full-grown. One day it will take over where we've left off.

Overtaken with happiness, forcing any trace of sadness that might ruin it away, we take the new pup to the bottom of the sea, along with its two-legs parent. We must bury the surface dweller. Our kin.

We are headed to the city at high speed. We are not slowed down by the weight of the pup or the two-legs. With determination, we plow through the water, diving through the icy depths. Blackness and cold welcome us.

The city we've built together with the other zoti aleyu thrums. Our body shakes from it, and it is the most welcome vibration. It has been one year since we left in search of where we came from.

When we are near enough that many will begin to hear and feel our approach, we slow down. What of this body? What would they think of it?

"I cannot bring this sadness to them," we say, and turn toward the outskirts, swimming deeper, to where there is ocean floor.

When a zoti aleyu dies, we bring it to shallow waters, where plant life grows, and wrap it in layers and layers of whatever we can find. Coral, seaweed, kelp. When it's done, the body is ovoid and thick, looking like a plumped, filled bag of waters. Or an entire womb. We then take it to some bit of seafloor and weigh it down with rocks.

We are prepared to do none of this with the two-legs, so we go to a small hut we've built outside the city and take off pieces of the wall to wrap the surface dweller in, till her form is concealed, so she may rot in some kind of peace if the ocean doesn't erode away the wrappings too quickly.

We set her off into a strong, cool current, saying farewell to our kin.

Over the years, we raise so many pups. We find more zoti aleyu. The strength of our people is our togetherness. Many of us lurk in the deep, yet we are one, and as the years pass and we grow old and decrepit, we remember that we are young, too, thriving, because we live on in this legacy of strange fish we've made.

In these last moments of our life, we try not to linger upon the horrors, of which there were many. We do not think about the secret of our origin and how easy it became to find zoti aleyu once we'd learned it.

We discovered which ships to follow. We memorized their routes. We learned their accents, their languages, and heard them through the water like an alarm. We followed ships where none went overboard, but this brought its own grief, for we knew the lives of those on the ship would not be good ones.

At times, we did more. We could not hide the truth of what happens on the ocean surface from all the zoti aleyu, many following us to discover our secret truth. The first such time, a group of them followed us and watched as a ship cast all of its cargo into the deep, the enslaved having been taken by some sickness. We and the other zoti aleyu now present gathered together to trouble the waters, to sink the ship. This did not come about by plan, but by anguish. As all of us wept and raged, we noticed the way our fury made the water pulse and rise. Swept up in the power of our newly discovered abilities, and engulfed by the grief over the immense loss of life, we let our ache fill the water. The effort of it left us and the other zoti aleyu spent for days, but when we recovered, we buried the bodies from the ship on the ocean floor.

We never wanted our people, our kindred, to suffer the loneliness we have known. Over the years, when others came to us desperate to talk about it, we encouraged them to forget. "Focus on what we have together. Here. Now." Not all could manage it, and they required extra help to let go of those terrible memories. We reached into their minds and searched, taking away the hurtful moments when we found them.

That is what we think about now, the peace we imparted, the togetherness we brought. We have absorbed many lifetimes of pain, but it is no matter compared to the good.

"Tell me a story," Aj says, fifty years old now. Hard to believe we witnessed his birth from the two-legged surface dweller, cast into the sea. "A happy one. Something that will comfort me in these next coming days, when I am to lose you, Amaba."

We nod. "I will tell you more than just a story. I will tell you every story. Happy and sad. But you must promise to tell no one else. I do not wish to burden them with these things I have to say. We cannot falter on our mission. Some things . . . weigh. I fear if they know the truth of everything, they will not be able to carry on, or they'll swim to the surface to learn things for themselves I do not want them to learn. Do you hear me?"

"I hear you, Amaba," Aj says.

"When I pass, you must tell them my wish for them," we say. "That they live lives of togetherness, in the present. That the many of them who started out their lives in loneliness and solitude, they must put it away, and remember where we are now. Together. Safe. Do you promise?"

"I promise," says Aj. "Now come on. Begin. Before it's too late."

"Do not forget any of this," we say, though our voice is weakening.

Aj touches his fins to ours, lays his cheek to our cheek. We communicate how pups communicate. In electricity, in charges. No need to speak. Aj sees all. Our memories transfer to him as we lived them.

We close our eyes in Aj's arms, listening to the water, to the noise of the city, to our kindred all around us.

There are so many of us now, we could hardly be called strange fish anymore. We have made a place in this sea. All the fluttering, building, loving, hunting, embracing, mating, we hear it all, our presence unmistakable. A whole chorus of the deep. *Wajinru*. We are not zoti aleyu. We are more vast and more beauteous than that name implies. We are a song, and we are together.

We remember.

5

YETU HURTLED THROUGH THE WATER, AWAY FROM the shadow of her people. Her tail fin jutted left and right to propel her to startlingly fast speeds. Her heart beat so fast, she couldn't tell one pulse from another. The steady thrum resounded like the hum of a whale.

She'd spent large swaths of time over the last year immobile, floating, lost in rememberings, and her body wasn't used to this level of performance. Muscle, fat, and cartilage had withered away, leaving behind a faint impression of what a wajinru should look like.

Yetu's will thrived where her body faltered. The only thought on her mind was go, go, go. Forward, never backward. Flee. The place she'd gone from was a world of pain, and there was no distance she could swim where that past wouldn't haunt her. Right now the wajinru were lost in the Remembrance, but they wouldn't always be, would they? Surely one among them would realize it was time to transfer the rememberings back, and that realization would spread. Without Yetu to signal when this was supposed to happen, it might take longer than usual, but not too long.

In such sparsely populated waters, Yetu stood out, her body creating unique patterns of waves that a wajinru tracker would be able to spot. The wajinru would come for her to return the rememberings once they recovered— and they would recover. Most assuredly they would. If Yetu could survive the rememberings intact, weak as she was, they could too.

She didn't let herself consider the possibility that they would be as lost in the face of it as she'd always been. To think such a thought for even half a moment would be to admit accursing them to immeasurable suffering. What if, like her, they all waned to shadows? Yetu shook her head. That wasn't going to happen. They would awaken and search for her so they could return the rememberings to their proper place. If she wanted to survive, she couldn't let that happen. They'd have to learn to adapt to them.

Yetu needed to go where they couldn't sense her, where they wouldn't search. She turned her body sharply upward and began her ascent to shallower waters. She was so tired that she put little effort into avoiding predators who could make easy work of her in her weakened, brain-addled state. All that mattered was escape.

She curled her body to make it move faster and faster,

and with each swim stroke she became more and more lightheaded. She wasn't sure she was breathing properly, or at all. Water glided over her gills, but it was different water than what she was used to. Had she risen higher in the ocean waters at a more reasonable rate, her body would've naturally adjusted, but she was swimming at top speeds.

The headache threatening at her temples was sharp and prickly. She didn't know what to do with the decreases in pressure. Her body felt wrong, like it was flying apart. There was nothing in these depths to hold her together, to squeeze her into place. As the light colored the water into a strange shade of dark, greenish blue, she closed her eyes, unused to the burn of sunshine.

This was familiar. She'd been here years and years ago. Words came to mind . . . hunting . . . hunting with Amaba. Or perhaps this place was from the History. She had a sense of the rememberings still, though already the details had faded. Whenever she tried to concentrate on anything specific, it slipped through her mind like sand through her webbed fingers. She could feel it still, but she didn't know it.

She couldn't say for sure where she'd seen the sunshine before, or this particular shade of blue. Random, meaningless images were all her mind dredged up. Where she'd once carried multitudes, there was sparsity.

Yetu was not so shallow yet that she felt out of danger. Light was only just beginning to penetrate. Some wajinru lived at these depths and would search for her here. She needed to go closer to the surface yet if she wanted to escape her people entirely.

Yetu pumped her body upward in a spiral, unthinkingly, too out of her mind to determine how far she was going. She guessed it had already been miles.

Light burned her eyes as she rose. Her pupils shrank to dots, but it was still too much. She couldn't focus on navigation with the headache that had spread from her temples to the top of her head all the way down to the base of her neck. Her sense of north, south, east, and west were gone. The currents were a maze. Unfamiliar animals moved in ways she didn't recognize.

Schools of fish flitted past her, turning her around. Which way was up again?

She followed the light, went toward its blinding whiteness. It was so warm. She'd never been this lost before, never been so unable to orient herself.

But Yetu didn't need to orient. She just needed to go. That was what mattered most. The goal was to be away from where she was now. The particulars of where she ended up were inconsequential.

She went up, up, and up until there was no up left, her head cracking through the sea's surface, oxygen from the air—the air!—blitzing her lungs. It made her remember fire and bombs, images of thrashing water tumbling through her mind, but then she couldn't remember where the fire and bombs came from. A few seconds later, Yetu couldn't remember what fire and bombs were.

Yetu was still. She let herself float. She'd left the

wajinru. That, she could not forget. She'd done the one thing the first historian wanted no wajinru to do. By leaving, Yetu was forcing them to endure the full weight of their History. She'd left them alone. Had abandoned them. They were not one people anymore. Yetu was apart. She squeezed her eyes shut against the light and reminded herself that they'd be okay. Amaba was the strongest wajinru Yetu had ever known. Her will did not bend. Not even the rememberings could ruin her.

Yetu trembled in the water, the physical ache of her desertion catching up to her. After everything, she still might die. She wasn't sure her body, debilitated from a year of neglect, could take what she'd done to it.

The light overhead was dimmer now. It still hurt to look at it with squinting eyes, but it wasn't as bad as she had imagined. The air was cold against Yetu's face. Sounds up here were different. She couldn't feel them properly. She turned around. Pink-orange haze crowned the sky.

Waves carried her up and down and toward the waning light. She bobbed, and she liked the rhythm of the subtle movement. She was, for the first time in many years, weightless.

Breaking through to the surface was not as new a feeling as she had expected it to be. Yetu had lived it all before through the rememberings, and though her mind struggled to focus on any particular image or memory, it was familiar. This was how her people must have felt after the Remembrance. The raw pain of the memories was gone, but the truth of it still remained in the wajinru, helping them to carry on.

That was how it had been before, at least. Now, her people were still remembering. It would take them some time to untangle themselves from it.

Yetu focused on making sense of her surroundings. There was nothing solid that she could see. No land. No boats. No birds. Just water and sky.

Soaking up the strange nothingness of life without the History, she drifted off to sleep. She awoke at random intervals, stoked to consciousness by the searing pain all over. When she tried to convince herself that she should go hunting for meat, she passed out again from fatigue and pain. This carried on for three days, her mind and body both at the brink.

Any attempts at wakefulness were quickly met with protest by her sore limbs. There was an ache, a throbbing, a pull, a tension in every part of her. She let herself be moved about the sea. Storms shook her, tossed her body like a piece of driftwood here and there. They lifted her, then thrust her back down.

Though pain racked over every inch of her, this was a deep, restful sleep. There were no nightmares. Rememberings didn't haunt her. She was just Yetu. She wasn't quite sure who that was, but she didn't mind the unknowing because it came with such calm, such a freedom from the pain.

When she finally awoke properly, it was onshore. And she wasn't alone.

* * *

The two-legs spoke a short distance away using a language Yetu couldn't name, but that she knew. She may
have forgotten the specifics of her own life and of the
rememberings she'd once carried, but in the same way she
still knew how to speak wajinru, she knew many other
languages too.

The surface dwellers were talking about her, asking
what she was, wondering among themselves if they'd
ever seen such a thing. One said that it didn't matter and
argued that Yetu looked more or less like food, and that
they should eat her.

Yetu groaned as she squinted her eyes open cautiously. The light was so unbearable, and pathetically, she
felt homesick already, coveting the deep sea, its blanket of
cold and dark.

One of the two-legs in the distance noted that Yetu
was moving, breathing. She'd washed into a small pool
bordered by massive rocks, the top half of her body in air,
the bottom in a mix of gushy sand that her torso seemed
to sink into. The water was extremely shallow, but the
tide brushed over her, back and forth, allowing her to
breathe through her gills.

Strangely, she was breathing with her mouth and nose,
too, sucking in air from her surroundings with the two
narrow slits in her face and her wide mouth. She didn't
know she could do that. It was a new, uncomfortable feeling, and her lungs felt unsatisfied.

Her body had never hurt this much before. The waves

must have battered her against the rocks before tossing her into this hole. All her cartilage was damaged.

One of the two-legs started to approach, and Yetu tried to move back into the water, but she was so stiff, so spent, and she certainly couldn't clear the large boulders separating her from the larger sea. She settled for a scream, opening her mouth wide, showing rows of sharp, long teeth, narrow and overlapping.

Her eyes and nose disappeared as her mouth expanded, her face replaced with a black, endless pit guarded by fangs. The two-legs jumped back, then stepped away farther and farther with cautious steps, hands held out in front of them.

She didn't quiet herself until they were a safe distance away, her teeth at the ready. She roared, the ensuing sound so different on land than it was in the water. She was pleased to find it sounded even more terrifying. She didn't want them to think they could hurt her just because she was in a vulnerable state. She would not let them forget she could tear them apart if she wanted to.

She swallowed air through her nose and chest, working out the mechanisms to suck it in so her chest didn't constantly feel empty. This made the surface dwellers stand back even farther. She must've looked hungry, like she was biting the air. As her breathing became more fluid, her body stilled and she could take in the sight of her audience more thoroughly.

There were four in total, and they looked similar enough that she guessed they were of the same people, perhaps even the same family. They were a range of sizes, and likely, ages, one small, coming only up to the hips of the others, one lanky and wobbly and uncertain on scrawny feet. They had dark brown skin and long, dark brown hair that was wild, scraggly, and long, matted into pieces that looked like long chunks of coral.

Yetu's memory stirred as she regarded them. At first, only a fuzzy gray outline emerged, then flashes of images from the History flicked through her mind without context. She saw the bodies of two-legs drowning, but not just in the water, on land, too. Water erupted from the sea and flowed onto the surface. A war. The ocean war? The wave war? Yetu concentrated deeply, straining to remember. Fractured details returned, but only briefly. The memories were caught in a quick current, hurriedly swishing away from her.

The drownings had been a part of the Tidal Wars— that was the name—a conflict between wajinru and two-legs. Yetu rummaged her mind for more images, more precise explanations, but it was all too disconnected to put together. She pressed and pressed, anxious to know what had happened, but all that was left of the rememberings were traces and impressions, and even those seemed to be fading from her. Though the curious quiet and lightness of her mind pleased her, she did not relish forgetting. She felt unmoored.

"What if it needs our help?" said the youngest one among them.

Yetu studied what remained of her scant memory to

identify the language they spoke, but even though she understood it with ease, she didn't know where it came from, what region of surface dwellers it belonged to. This, very much like the breathing through her mouth and nose, surprised her. How much of two-leggedness was in her? She didn't know what came from instinct and what came from the History and echoes of rememberings.

Though Yetu knew that at least distantly the two-legs were kin, the similarities were not as prominent as their differences. Yetu was black and scaled. She lived in the water and she looked it. They looked so . . . fleshy. Yetu only had skin like theirs over her belly, and a smaller portion on her face, over her eyes, nose, and mouth.

"Leave it. Let's go," said another one of the two-legs.

They left, and she was alone again. Yetu still couldn't move. Sunlight faded, thank goodness. She welcomed the dark and the rising tide, which soon left her gloriously submerged.

Strangely, despite the physical pain her body was in, she felt better than she had in ages. The ache of her muscles, bones, and cartilage was nothing compared to the pain she was used to carrying, of the History and what they'd been through. There was no doubt that despite the disorientation of life without the rememberings, Yetu felt tranquility, too.

Not far off from sleep, she wondered if she'd still be here in the morning, or if she'd wash up on a different, nearby shore. How miraculous it was to go where she pleased. No past, and no future, either. Before leaving the History, she'd had little chance to discover who plain old Yetu was. The wajinru inside her from the past had pulled her backward, and the wajinru around her had pulled her outward toward their various ends. The combating forces had stretched her so far this way and that way that she had lost her shape. If she had a will of her own, she was too deflated to actually exercise it. Now, though, reduced to a skeleton, she could build herself back up however she wanted.

Prior to this Remembrance, the other wajinru must've felt this way all the time. Unburdened, they could do as they pleased and follow their whims wherever they took them. Now, trapped in the mud womb, they had to endure the limitations Yetu had had since she was fourteen.

As Yetu drifted in the tidal pool toward sleep, she couldn't shake the feeling that she had cursed them. After all, when she held the rememberings, only one wajinru suffered. In the aftermath of her leaving, all of them did. All but Yetu. That wasn't right, but neither was the alternative. She didn't deserve to die, did she?

The wajinru weren't faring well, Yetu had no doubt of that, but eventually, hunger and fatigue would draw them out of the trance. They'd carry the rememberings, but they'd be able to resume hunting and live the rest of their lives.

Yetu watched the ocean. Waves collided with the surface at regular intervals, water spraying. Overhead, clouds gathered. The seas were not particularly rough nor the sky particularly gray, but a heavy rain was on the horizon.

It meant nothing. Storms came and went for any number of reasons. It wasn't a sign anything was amiss, that the wajinru were worrying the water. Still, Yetu kept guard over the water, eyes steady on the sea as she succumbed to sleep. Everything would be all right now that she was free.

Yetu next awoke to the smell of dead fish. A pile of fifteen of them lay next to her on the beach, their tails tied together with a piece of browned, twined seaweed.

She recognized it for the gift it was and devoured it. She slept again.

The next day, there was more. Still hungry from having eaten so poorly over the last year, she devoured it too. There were blacktails among the bounty, one of her amaba's favorites. She was about to call out to invite her to join the meal before she remembered that Amaba was not here. Yetu chewed the fish slowly, hesitant to take another bite. While she feasted on gifts from a stranger, Amaba and the other wajinru were trapped in rememberings. They would recover in time, Yetu had to believe that, but without her guidance, they were surely stumbling and scared.

Reminded of the heavy rain in the distance, a rain that would not touch the corner of the earth where she was settled, Yetu looked out to the ocean. When *would* the wajinru wake up from the trance of the Remembrance? They didn't have that much time before they'd work themselves into the same kind of state Ayel had when the

Remembrance had first started and she'd forgotten who she was. Without direction, they'd break open the walls of the mud womb, leaving themselves exposed, and the world in danger. Taken by rage and grief from the rememberings, and without the cognizance to hold themselves back, the wajinru all together could stir the ocean waters to a degree that would disrupt the natural weather cycles. The winds, the skies—they'd both be electrified into a whipping frenzy. The wajinru could make a storm as big as the one that prickled like a half memory in the back of Yetu's mind, the one that drowned the land.

It wouldn't come to that. Yetu worried because that was what she always did, prone to fits of anxiousness and over-reactivity. She shook her head and took another bite of fish. She forced herself to swallow it after realizing she'd been chewing the same morsel for several minutes.

The vastness of the ocean looked so different from above, so much less comprehensible. Its murky blue waters were a dark veil separating her from her people. Cut off from them, she had trouble making sense of who or what she was. Without them, she seemed nothing more than a strange fish, alone. Absent the rememberings, who was she but a woman cast away?

Yetu squeezed her eyes shut against the light of sunrise. She had not been granted stillness like this since she was a child. Never had she had so much time to think. She wasn't even sure she could do it.

Another day passed, and the next morning, when she awoke to fish, she saw the person who'd left her the food just as they were walking away. Yetu whimpered to grab their attention, and the two-legs turned around, startling back a few feet as they took in the sight of her.

"Hi, there, fishy fish," they said. "Shh, now. Quiet. I'm Suka, and I'm not going to do anything to hurt you." They were one of the original four who'd seen her the day she had first become beached.

"It's all right," they said, holding out their hands to placate her. She recognized the same gesture as one her amaba did sometimes. Was such a thing passed down in DNA? Was it a part of the History she'd never noticed before? She went to flick through the rememberings in her head to find previous instances of it, but—she had no rememberings anymore, not like she used to. When she reached for the past, nothing was there. The emptiness inside her stretched far and wide in every direction like a cavern. It was lonely. She had thought herself unmoored when she was the historian, but this did not compare. She was a blip.

"I promise, all right? I promise I'm not going to hurt you," Suka said. "Not that I could if I tried. I know you can't possibly understand me but— Everything's all right. I promise."

She believed them, that they weren't going to hurt her. After all, they'd given her all this food. But Suka didn't seem like an authority to trust on whether everything was going to be all right or not. They didn't know anything about her. They didn't know what she'd swum from.

"I understand you," Yetu said, the words spitting up from her throat unexpectedly and in an odd configuration. She sounded croaky and rough; her voice so deep she wasn't sure the two-legs would understand. She had never spoken this language before, and the words felt strange sliding against her esophagus and tongue. The words tickled faintly against her skin, but not in the same way they would were she in the water.

Everything about life on land strained her senses. It was disorienting to use her eyes rather than her skin. She was like a newborn, cast away from its amaba and grasping outward for anything solid on which to hold.

"My god, my god, my god," Suka said. "You are— What are you?"

Yetu breathed deeply in, but it just rattled her more, the oddness of getting oxygen through the air rather than the water.

"Thank you for the fish," she said. "I'm recovering from a difficult journey and unable to hunt for myself."

Suka looked at her in silence, their eyes wide and mouth agape, showing the tips of what looked like very useless, blunt teeth.

"I am Yetu," she said, hoping that might calm them.

"You speak. You're alive," said Suka, trembling.

"If you didn't think I was alive before, why did you bring food to sustain me?" Yetu asked.

"I meant you're . . . you're like us," Suka said.

It was flattering to be thought of in those terms. As

similar. As sharing something in common with not just one other, but a whole *us*. Since she was fourteen, she'd always been marked as different by her role as historian.

Yetu squeezed her eyes shut, regretting the thought. She wasn't ready to be swept into the fold of a stranger. She was wajinru, no matter how far away they were from her. Being historian, being different, didn't change that. "I didn't mean to startle you so. I only wanted to thank you for the fish," she said.

Suka calmed, limbs visibly loosening. "It actually wasn't me. It's Oori who's been catching them for you. I just, I happened to be here."

"Oori. Is that one of your siblings?" asked Yetu. "One of the . . . people . . . from the other day?" The words were much more fluid in her mind than they were coming from her mouth. It sounded like she was belching them out.

"No. Oori fishes around here, but she's not family," Suka said. "She's from an island off the northwestern coast. We're inland mainland folk, and much farther south. I'd say she trades with us, but to be honest, mostly she just gives. I tried to give her a blanket once and she laughed at me and asked if I'd mistaken her for an infant, so. That's Oori."

"Can you tell Oori thank you for me? Then tell her I'd like more?"

"More?"

"More fish. Or preferably a seal. Something fatty."

"Oori is—she doesn't take kindly to requests or

demands on her time," said Suka, like it wasn't something to be wary of about her. Yetu found the quality fascinating. She wanted to be a person who didn't take kindly to requests, who knew her own mind. Maybe if she'd had a stronger will, she'd have been able to resist the pull of the ancestors, able to carry the History without so much grief.

"That's admirable," said Yetu. "It was only a question. Not a demand. She should do what she wants."

"Oh, she does."

Despite what Suka warned, Oori did bring bigger loads of fish over the next few days. And fresh seal. Small sharks. King mackerel.

Yetu swam in tiny circles in the pool in an attempt to keep herself awake for longer hours. She wanted to catch a glimpse of this Oori. The tightness of her temporary resting quarters was stifling, but the border of boulders formed an appealing bubble around her, shutting out the sensations of the ocean. She'd tire of the curious blankness against her skin compared to the open sea eventually; for now, she lapped up the calm, the finiteness of it. As long as she didn't make a point to tune her skin to the waters beyond the wall, her world ended but a few feet from wherever she was. It was a cage, but also a protective cocoon.

On the third day of trying to spot Oori, Yetu finally did. She awoke when the sky was only just turning light, a pleasing dark blue shade that reminded Yetu of being underwater where sunlight barely reached.

"I see you," Yetu said, using a wajinru greeting.

Yetu heard a startled splash.

"So?" Oori said, her voice quiet, deep, and raspy.

"I was just letting you know," said Yetu, alert now. It was too dark to properly see her, and sound didn't travel as well through air. She could neither feel nor hear the shape of this strange woman beyond a vague outline.

"I suppose now I know," said Oori.

"Thank you for the food," Yetu said, swimming closer to where Oori stood in the pool, slowed down by the shallowness of the water.

"It's nothing," Oori said, the gruffness in her voice showing no signs of retreating.

"It's food. It's helping me get better."

"What should I have done instead? Not provide what is necessary? Don't take it to heart. I fed my mother till the day she died, and I despised her. Good-bye."

Their conversations over the next several days continued to be short. Oori had no interest in Yetu, nor in anyone, it seemed. She spent her days out on the water in a wooden sailboat Yetu had spotted, which, given the calm winds of late, had become more of a paddleboat. She spent nights on the water as well, sleeping in her boat, the rope tied to a large boulder. According to the others, she didn't always tie herself to shore, letting the water carry her wherever it would, living off fish and stores of ocean.

"I wish there was a way to properly thank her," Yetu said to Suka one day.

"Who? Oori?"

"Yes. Who else?" asked Yetu.

"She doesn't like to be thanked. That's too close to kinship for her, which she doesn't do."

"Well, kinship isn't inherently a good thing," said Yetu, beginning to understand Oori more and more. Perhaps for Oori, kinship meant taking care of a mother who'd hurt her. For Yetu, it had meant isolation from her people as she tried to cope with the rememberings. And now? She wasn't sure what it meant. She would always see herself as wajinru. That was one thing she'd figured out since being in the tidal pool. The sea beckoned her, and it pained her not to join it, to be one with it, to feel it all over her. Even though it often hurt, her skin relished the pressure and the feedback. Above the surface, everything seemed so insubstantial and light. She missed being a part of not just the sea, but the whole world. Without the History, she felt out of place and out of time. She missed being connected to all.

But connection came with responsibility. Duty choked independence and freedom. If Oori didn't want kinship, Yetu could understand. Why be beholden to anyone else's agenda? Oori was obligated to herself and herself alone.

"I just mean that she's different, you know? Not like us. She's not so good with, hm, how do you say, human interaction and any trappings of decorum or rules. I suppose that's why she prefers animals to people. Most animals don't exchange hellos and ask how the other is. They just exist next to one another."

Yetu's ears and skin perked at the sound of that. Oori preferred animals, did she?

"Perfect, then. I'm not human," said Yetu. Though her foremothers were two-legs, she felt she had very little in common with these strange land walkers, whose teeth were weak and flat. "I am animal."

Suka played with their breath in the back of their throat then pushed it through their mouth—a strange habit of the two-legs. It was too thoughtful to be a sigh. Too calm and content to be a groan. Just a sound, meaningless, as they considered what to say.

"Yes, but only animal-ish?" they said, hedging.

Yetu didn't understand what that could mean. She groaned, unable to keep track of it all. Without the vivid images of the rememberings, she was left only with outlines of memories, and even those were waning. Two-legs had specific ways of classifying the world that Yetu didn't like. She remembered that, at least. They organized the world as two sides of a war, the two-legs in conflict with everything else. The way Suka talked about farming, it was as if they ruled the land and what it produced, as opposed to—they'd just said it themselves—existing alongside it.

Suka didn't understand Oori. Yetu did. And what she didn't understand, she wanted to. Suka had written Oori off. But Yetu was happy to simply exist alongside her whenever Oori made herself available for such things.

The first time Oori stayed longer than a few moments, Yetu got to see her in the sunlight. She had dark skin, darker even than Suka's, and there were scars and markings cut into her face in elaborate patterns. They were beautiful and strangely familiar. Yetu squinted to get a stronger impression, but she couldn't place them. Something from the History? That didn't feel right. The memory felt more present than that, more recent.

Yetu wanted nothing more than to keep looking at Oori's face, which was startlingly captivating. Her eyes were dark as the deep. Yetu drew her into a conversation about fish bait so she might keep looking upon her. Oori remained for nearly an hour debating the merits of this and that technique. Yetu felt bereft when she left, and she spent the rest of the day coming up with topics that might bid Oori to stay even longer.

The next day, Yetu taught Oori how to better read the winds as they related to the currents. For that lesson, Oori remained the whole morning and part of the afternoon. The next day, Yetu opened up about her thoughts on fishing nets, how sometimes, when she was a pup, she'd sneak off and tear all of them to shreds with her teeth. Oori listened, eyes toward the sea but ears toward Yetu, then asked if all nets were the same or were some worse than others. Yetu could talk about this topic at length, and she did, Oori never once standing up to leave. She nodded at random intervals and asked clarifying questions, but was otherwise content to hear what Yetu had to say.

A week passed, and Yetu ran out of topics, but Oori remained anyway. She told Yetu that despite her comfort on the ocean, she got seasick still. She loved riding waves on her little boat. She loved to swim. She could hold her breath for three minutes, which Yetu understood was supposed to be a significant amount of time for a two-legs.

When the both of them ran out of things to say and Oori looked like she might be getting up to leave, Yetu convinced her to stay by saying that there was a special sound she could make to attract certain types of fish to her. It was a hiccupping whistle, a gentler, more musical version of a seabird's call. It had a hypnotizing effect, for one, but also stimulated pleasure centers in many creatures' brains when combined with an electrical signal that wajinru could project.

"Like this?" Oori asked, making the sound in the air.

"Close," said Yetu, but it wasn't really, not at all. Her vocal apparatus was too different from a wajinru's. "Make the sound in the water. See if that works."

Oori hesitated, unsure for several moments. She was currently in a full squat on one of the boulders that surrounded the tidal pool, heels to ground, bottom nearly touching the rock.

"Come," said Yetu. "Come here now."

Yetu relished all the time she got to see Oori in the bright light of day. In addition to the patterned divots and scars, there were black markings inked permanently into her face and neck in similarly elaborate designs. If only Yetu could feel them, she might know what they were. Her eyes did not see as well as her scales did.

Oori's voice and manner reminded Yetu of her amaba, stern and insistent. Yetu glanced toward the wide sea.

Amaba's suffering must've been so great right now, left for days in the seizing chokehold of the History. Yetu's breath caught at the thought of it. Even if Amaba and the others had risen from the trance, it would take them some time to carry on life as usual.

Yetu tried to tune her skin to the water, to feel past the boulders out into the larger ocean. Thousands of sensations brushed up against her, but they were all whisper soft, and she couldn't distinguish the wajinru from any other living creatures in the deep. Was it wishful thinking to hope that meant they were out of the Remembrance and had moved on now, living quiet, unremarkable lives?

Yetu returned her eyes to Oori, and Oori sat down on her bottom. She let her legs fall into the tidal pool, swaying her feet back and forth.

"See, it's nice, isn't it? Come in," Yetu said.

"It's cold," said Oori, but it was just an excuse. Oori was not the sort to be put off by a slight chill. She braved the open sea daily, her boat crashing over waves that sprayed her with buckets of icy water.

"I don't believe you have ever felt cold in your life," said Yetu, gently chiding. "Come now. Get in."

Yetu didn't know what had come over her. She hadn't had a conversation like this since before she'd taken on the History. She hadn't teased or been teased since she was thirteen.

A lonely child, more easily hurt than other wajinru, she'd always tended to keep to herself. But before becoming historian, she could be with people at least, talk to them and confide in them. Once she had taken on the rememberings, she'd lost that ability, too gripped by the past to do more than the bare minimum to interact in the present.

She'd come to prize solitude over all else, desperate for quiet and a stop to the voices of the past and present alike. Friends she'd held dear disappeared, put off by her emotional distance, her unpredictability.

"Please?" said Yetu, keeping her voice light, playful. She hoped she was doing it right. She hoped that she didn't sound too childish, trying to replicate her manner as a child because that was the last time she'd attempted to make conversation with someone she liked so much.

Oori groaned softly and shortly, but gave no indication that she was truly upset by Yetu's encouragement. "I *was* cold once," she said, "and I didn't like it. I aim never to feel it again."

Yetu tingled all over. She'd never been so content to talk to someone before. In fact, over the last twenty years, she'd avoided talking at all except those times when it was absolutely necessary . . . and even then. During her earliest Remembrances, she'd stayed silent the entire ceremony, providing no filter for the painful images she had sent her people.

"It feels wonderful. Come. Please," Yetu pleaded again. She hoped she wasn't pushing Oori too far. Yetu knew what it was like to be torn between one's own wants and the wants of others.

"Fine," said Oori, rolling her eyes. She slid into the

water but kept her distance from Yetu, who was on the other side of the pool. It hadn't occurred to Yetu before that Oori might've been afraid of her.

"Do I frighten you?" asked Yetu. She was glad that her voice sounded so strange, croaky, and broken, because it disguised any hurt or bitterness in it. "Scared that even though you've been feeding me, talking to me, that I'll gobble you up? You think so little of me?" She'd meant it to sound like a joke, but she knew it didn't come out that way.

Oori didn't break under Yetu's questions. Her face was still and calm, like the deep itself. "You are something from the wild. It isn't a matter of thinking little of you. It's a matter of common sense and respect. If I were to nurse a shark back to health, I would keep my distance when releasing it. I don't know anything about you. What if you have an insatiable need to bite anything that is within two meters of you? What if you have the prey drive of a lion?"

Yetu didn't know what a lion was. "I don't. And besides, you look disgusting to eat."

Oori caressed the top of the water with her right palm, sending tiny shocks of waves over Yetu's skin a short distance away in the water. "Still. It remains that I know nothing about you. Would you trust a strange creature so readily? Don't you harbor some recognition that I might do you harm? If you don't, you are naive."

"I am not naive," said Yetu. "I know more about the world's cruelty than you ever will. I know all of it."

Except she didn't anymore. The rememberings were gone, replaced with a ghost. Still, the echoes the History had left told her that the two-legs were capable of savagery.

"Oh really? What do you know, Yetu the wise?" asked Oori.

"I know what it feels like to be drowned," she said, refusing to explain more, because she couldn't remember more. Her only recollection of it was the sensation in her lungs. "I won't be able to show you how to make the proper sound if you don't come closer. Don't you want to lure all the fish to you?"

Yetu dipped her head in and hoped Oori would do the same. She did, but it took her a whole minute. "Go like this," said Yetu in wajinru, before realizing that wouldn't make sense to Oori. She switched to her language and said the same, then demonstrated the sound. Oori pushed back up through the water to take a breath, then came down again and tried to emulate the sound.

Yetu shook her head, then gestured for Oori to join her back above the water. "Don't use your mouth so much. The sounds are through your throat. Try screaming. Or screeching. That will get you closer." Yetu hoped she wasn't being too demanding. It felt good to share something freely with another. She could think of all kinds of things she wanted to show Oori. "Come now. Again."

This time, the sound Oori made under the water was half decent, and though it didn't sound like any word

Yetu knew, at least it sounded like it could be a word in wajinru.

Oori emerged from the water looking very pleased with herself. She wasn't smiling, but Yetu detected the satisfied smugness there. "Now it's your turn," said Yetu.

"My turn?"

"To show me something. Isn't that how it works?" Conversations, shared moments—they were exchanges, were they not? This was what Yetu remembered of them from the time when her life had been a little more social than it was now.

"I have nothing to show you," said Oori. "The only thing I know is the water, and I doubt I know anything about it that you don't know better and more deeply."

Yetu didn't doubt it either. "Well, you could tell me about something else. You could tell me something about yourself."

"What do you want to know?" asked Oori, looking more comfortable in the water now. She watched the sea, and birds flying overhead, and crabs in the sand. Her eyes never once met Yetu's.

"Where are you from?" Yetu asked, hoping she'd get a chance to ask another question too. If she didn't, and she'd wasted her question on something as mundane as place of origin, she'd regret it dearly. She wanted to know what Oori wanted more than anything else in the world, and what she was most afraid of, and had she ever been brought to shivers from sadness or anger. Did she like Yetu? Would she have treated any creature who washed up into this pool so gently, or was Yetu special?

"I am from a dead place," Oori said.

"What do you mean?"

"The land is dead. The people are dead."

"Your parents?" asked Yetu.

"Dead."

"Siblings?"

"Dead," said Oori.

"Kin?"

"All dead. I am the last of the Oshuben," said Oori.

Yetu looked for traces of sadness on Oori's face but found none. She was blank.

"What an unspeakable loss," said Yetu, not wishing to assume that Oori's stern countenance revealed anything about how she felt on the matter. According to Amaba, Yetu simply looked "away" and "removed" at times when she was experiencing some of the most violent rememberings.

"I can't imagine a hole as wide as that," said Yetu, looking out at the sea. When she made her skin receptive to it, she swore she could feel the wajinru's anguished weeping through the water. It was like fish crawling all over her skin.

It wasn't real, though. Just her imagination. Through the rocks, it was difficult to feel the wider ocean.

The ocean looked calm, but in the distance, she felt the sort of heavy rain and winds that signaled a coming storm. It was too far away to see how big it was, or which direction it was moving. If they had broken from the mud womb and decided to rise, the wajinru could cause a storm like that, couldn't they? They all possessed the electrical capability to move the waters.

Yetu shook her head. She had no evidence that was going on. Wild speculation wouldn't serve her. It was just another way to tie her to the past, and the past had been responsible for nearly killing her.

She'd learned how to deal with the rememberings. The other wajinru would too, in time.

"I am sorry for what happened to you, for all that was taken from you," said Yetu. Even though she'd left her family, Yetu didn't like to think of her amaba not existing. Such a thought was intolerable.

"It's the way things go," said Oori.

It was, and Yetu knew no words to console her. "Is there anyone to enact vengeance upon?"

"Everyone and no one," Oori said, inching forward through the water closer to Yetu.

"Sometimes it's not the worst thing to lose everything. Sometimes it's good," said Yetu, thinking that for the first time in twenty years, she could feel the ocean now without it overwhelming her senses.

She had room to think. To know what she wanted and believed. And all it had cost her was everything.

"Good?" asked Oori. Her steely facade cracked, but only infinitesimally. Yetu wondered if she'd even seen it at all. She felt the brokenness of Oori's voice against her skin, but that was the only sign.

"If the past is full of bad things, if a people is defined by the terror done to them, it's good for it to go, don't you think?" said Yetu. "I was a historian." It made her feel so good to say that. *Was.* No longer. She blinked her eyes shut and tried to cast out thoughts of the wajinru locked in the Remembrance. "It was a very holy thing for my kind. It meant I held on to all the memories so no one else had to, generations and generations of them. Six hundred years of pain."

"Were you like a storyteller then?" asked Oori.

Yetu shook her head. "All the memories of those who've come before, they lived inside me. Real as flesh. I remembered them like they were my own. I walked inside them."

Oori nodded, curious and intrigued. "Touched by spirits," she said sagely.

"By electricity," Yetu countered. "And it hurts. I gave up the memories so I could be free."

So she could live.

Oori looked out at the sea, unblinking. "I would take any amount of pain in the world if it meant I could know all the memories of the Oshuben. I barely know any stories from my parents' generation. I can't remember our language. How could you leave behind something like that? Doesn't it hurt not to know who you are?"

"I know who I am now. All I knew before was who they were, who they wanted me to be," said Yetu. "And it was killing me. It *did* kill me. I wasn't Yetu. I was just a shell for their whims."

Oori shook her head and stood up from the water. "But your whole history. Your ancestry. That's who you are."

"No. I am who I am now. Before, I was no one. When you're everyone in the past, and when you're for everyone in the present, you're no one. Nobody. You don't exist. I didn't exist. If you prefer a world where I don't exist, then stop bringing me fish."

"Fine," said Oori, turning to leave. The water splashed, brushing Yetu's skin. She hated that despite being as angry as she was at Oori, she was thrilled by even that small amount of connection with her. These feelings were unfamiliar. More than anything, she wanted Oori near, but Yetu yelled at her to go.

"You are nothing but a silly fish," said Oori. "Of course you wouldn't understand the importance of having a history."

Oori did not come back for three days.

6

History was everything. Yetu knew that. But it wasn't kind. Abandoned now by Oori, Yetu dwelled in the darkest parts of it. Not *the* History. That was all but gone. Her own history, the once upon a time when she'd been fourteen, small, and totally unequipped to handle the darkness she had been a host to.

She remembered Amaba shouting at her, as she'd started doing a lot in that time, because Yetu was supposed to go practice-hunting with some young girls in the nearby den but had been away in a remembering and had forgotten.

When she awoke, she refused to go.

"I can't see them anymore," Yetu cried. The same way that Amaba was always shouting, Yetu was always weeping.

"It's been weeks since you've seen anyone. You cannot

prefer this loneliness," Amaba insisted. She was right, in her own way. It wasn't a preference but a necessity to keep out the pain. "Go, right now! Go to them, or else."

But Yetu revealed a shark tooth in her front fin and held it to her neck. "I'd rather die than go."

At fourteen, the rush of rememberings from the History had been so new that they suffocated her.

"My child," Amaba said, frightened. "What sickness is this? What madness would cause one to put oneself in fatal harm purposely, knowingly? Surely, it cannot exist."

Yetu turned from Amaba and toward the dark fold of infinite ocean beckoning her from all sides. There were pockets of the deep still untouched by sentient life. Yetu had ached for them. For their quiet.

"What of your responsibilities to us, to the wajinru?" Amaba added. "Without you, we perish. Without the Remembrance and the gift of the memories you bestow on us annually, we would flounder until there was nothing left of us but cartilage."

Yetu swam in pacing circles, speed increasing with each repetition, still clutching the shark fin. No amount of explanation would make Amaba understand what it was like to have the rememberings. The two of them had been here before, and before, and before.

With each twist of her body, she churned the water into thick, impenetrable blurs. It was a maelstrom to hide in, Amaba's words unable to pierce.

"Still yourself. Now," Amaba said, reaching her front

fins through the dense cloud to touch her child. "And drop that thing!"

Yetu, small for a wajinru of fourteen years, slipped from her amaba's grip and continued her efforts to spin, mouth catching up to tail. Moving was the only way to quiet the restless energy burning through her like electric cancer.

"Such madness does exist," Yetu said, dizzy, her words gobbled up by the eddy she was whirring. "You all made me this way. I carry the burden of remembering so you don't have to. So acknowledge it, then! That it's a burden!"

Amaba tackled Yetu from above, wrapping her fins around her child's torso and curling her tail fin around Yetu's to immobilize it. "Still, child. Still," she said.

"You're always wanting answers to why I do the things I do, but when I try to give them, you cannot fathom it. Is this my curse? To be unfathomable? Am I even alive anymore? Maybe Yetu is already dead," said Yetu. "Are you even holding me now, Amaba? Or are you holding a corpse?"

Amaba pressed the webbed appendages at the ends of her fins over Yetu's face as she let out a moaning cry. "Stop it. Don't speak such ugliness."

But Yetu couldn't keep silent, not now that the truth was gushing out of her so freely. "All I have is ugliness, Amaba. All I have are these ugly rememberings. You say madness such as mine doesn't exist, but it would exist in you, too, if you had to experience the ugly things I do all the time," she said, defeated and deflated in her amaba's arms, near suffocation. Amaba held her so tight, she couldn't sway her body enough to filter water.

"What about the rememberings could be so, so maddening?" Amaba asked. Yetu tried to writhe free, but Amaba's strength was irrefutable. "Tell me, child!" Amaba said.

"Dying," Yetu cried out. The pair was jowl to jowl as Amaba overpowered Yetu from behind. "Today I was three boys in the moments before their deaths, then I was them during their deaths. They were three bodies and then they burst from the inside into thousands and thousands of little, incomplete bodies. I know what it's like to be turned into splinters and fragments."

Amaba shook her head forcefully, the rushing echo of water against Yetu's skin enough to make her wish she was inside of one of the rememberings now, rather than here, because when you are in pain, sometimes the only escape is another different pain.

"Why are you telling me these horrible things?" her amaba asked.

"They're true."

"They are not. Such a thing—what could even cause that? Such breaking apart of bodies?"

"Energy," Yetu said.

Oblong slivers of cartilage, seared skin, tooth shards—Yetu had learned so much about the past since taking on the History, but she'd learned about the present, too. Her amaba didn't want to believe that the things Yetu spoke about the past were true. If they were, what would it say about her as a parent to have consented to her child becoming a vessel of such ugliness?

"Stop, stop, stop, child," cried Amaba. She swam away, putting as much distance between herself and Yetu as she could. She could not even look at her.

"I tell the rememberings to stop," said Yetu. "But they don't. So why should I stop for you?"

Frothy water spewed from Amaba's mouth as she made gurgled, choked noises. This was why Yetu was to remain silent about the things she knew. These rememberings, these secrets of their History, were for Yetu and Yetu only.

It was at this age that Yetu first considered abandoning the History all together. All wajinru could live in peace, unburdened by the past. No more historian.

But when she brought her ideas to her amaba and other wajinru, they scolded her for her blasphemy. A people needed a history. To be without one was death. This was a feeling they knew all too well when the Remembrance drew near. It was an ache for knowing, and Yetu had had it once too.

Those years were far behind her, but still, she could not shake the memories. Sulky and scared, she had spent most of her youth feeling abandoned by the wajinru, even when they most tried to show their love.

Amaba held a gathering in Yetu's honor once, certain that that was all her daughter needed to perk up, to become the old Yetu again. Slightly sensitive, yes, but loving and warm.

"We don't have much time. People will be arriving soon," said Amaba. Yetu had been instructed to hunt meat for the get-together. Amaba fluttered off to make her own preparations, fully expectant that her daughter would do as she was told. Yetu, though, was far past an age where she blindly followed her amaba's commands. That would've been true even without the History inside of her. Absent the rememberings that aged and embittered her, she would've yearned to know herself as just Yetu. Who was she outside of her relationship to her kin?

Still, Yetu swam off to hunt, using this new freedom Amaba had granted to do something she'd been meaning to do since her failed suicide attempt. The prey she was after was not for meat. It was for a sacrifice.

It was only a short time before the gathering would begin. Yetu needed to locate a worthy animal, kill it, and do the ceremony, all before anyone was the wiser.

Amaba didn't like "that nonsense" as she called it. Her only god was Yetu herself. Her only religion, the History. She showed her devotion by ensuring its preservation in her child.

But through the rememberings, Yetu had seen the many ways throughout time that the wajinru had communed with the world beyond knowledge. One way was to offer blood to the ocean, and in that blood, there was truth—if one knew how to look.

Yetu swam quietly, smoothly, with no extraneous strokes of her tail. She tended to be a distinctive swimmer, sometimes twisting and turning her body into a swirl pattern as she pulsed forward. The result was a wake identifiable by other wajinru who knew her. Today, she didn't want to be found.

The best prey lived a little shallower than where she and her amaba were currently staking out the waters, but there were more wajinru higher up too. There was more potential for her to be discovered, especially because wajinru would be nearby to get to Amaba's gathering.

Yetu kept her nerve endings poised as she carried out the hunt. She wanted something big. Something old. The easy answer was a shark, but they were more difficult to find this deep, and she didn't want to have to go too close to the surface.

That left squid. Clever and therefore difficult prey. She didn't have time for that.

Then she caught a wisp of it on her skin. Something gargantuan moving, perhaps a mile away from her, several hundred meters closer to the surface than she.

She swam toward it, disguising her identity by fluttering her webbed fins and blowing bubbles in interesting shapes and patterns so her prey might think she was only a school of deepwater fish.

As she got closer, the creature's contours became clearer. She could just begin to make out what it was. Something strange. Something she didn't see often.

Yes, yes, she could see it now, feel it on her skin. A frilled shark. Perfection. She swam decisively toward it, realizing speed now was more important than anything else. In the dark, it wouldn't be able to see her well. She rarely saw the frilled shark this deep. It'd be less used to the complete blackness.

She'd come on it like a sudden current from underneath. Open her jaw and crush its throat. Swimming faster and faster, she was almost there. She bared her teeth. She reached out her fins, more flexible at the base than any sharks, and grabbed hold.

They were belly to belly, her arms wrapped around it. She plunged her teeth inside its tough skin and shook her head to undo its flesh.

The creature shook and writhed, trying to throw her off, but the appendages at the end of her front fins had suckers that stuck to its scales. It didn't take long for it to die.

She pressed her teeth into those places where the arteries were juiciest and most prominent, then let the blood drain from it. She let the blood cover her. In lighter seas, she'd have appeared pink with it.

Yetu had never done anything like this before. She'd only seen this precise ritual once in her rememberings.

She exsanguinated it, then danced her body in swirling circles to mix it into a torrent, a miniature hurricane. When she was so dizzy she couldn't carry on, she was to carry on anyway, submerged in the red lifewater of this ancient creature.

And she was to put all her wills, all her intentions, into telling the ancestors that this was an offering for them, so they might reveal themselves to her and grant her what she desired.

What she desired was to be free of the History.

Yetu was so ill from spinning that she was on the verge of vomiting. Thankfully, her stomach was largely empty.

She near passed out in the blood, and from above, the frilled shark body began to come down on her. She tried her mightiest to push the heavy beast away, and she finally did. More blood came from it. That was why it wasn't working. The ceremony required every last bit.

She squeezed arteries with her fins. The smell was sickening and metallic all around her.

"Historian!"

Amaba?

"Historian!"

It was many wajinru, her amaba among them.

Several came toward her in the water screaming her name, her title.

Through the chorus, Yetu singled out the voice of her amaba, but instead of calling her by her name, she said *historian*.

Yetu was too sick to attempt to escape their scrutiny. She didn't want to remember how she'd failed to live up to the standards of the previous historians, who had carried the History without complaint.

She was a failure. The ancestors hadn't come to grant her anything. The only wajinru here were the live ones.

Yetu floated in a black, heavy haze of bloody ocean as she lay in wait. When the wajinru came, she could feel their racing hearts, their scrunched noses.

All could smell the uncharacteristic carnage of such a large creature drained of all blood. All could feel the strange, thin texture of blood in the otherwise dense seawater. All could feel maddened energy crackling off Yetu, and they were scared.

"Why would you bring all these people to me, Amaba?" Yetu asked. Her voice was so low and without energy that she wasn't sure her amaba would hear it.

"My sweet child, why wouldn't I?" she asked.

Yetu groaned. Was it the nausea, the crowd of frightened wajinru floating in a circle around her, or her amaba's refusal to accept that she was not her sweet little girl anymore?

"I will send them away. We will go home," said Amaba, perhaps apologetic for insisting on this gathering that had brought so many people near.

Amaba did what she could to soothe Yetu, but the problem was that she could not share in this tragedy. She could not share Yetu's loneliness. All she could do was stroke her tremoring, sob-wrecked body.

There was no saving Yetu.

7

Oori finally did come back three days later, but Yetu didn't feel as happy by her return as she thought she would. Left alone to stew in her past—the past Oori insisted was so meaningful and important and good—she felt tender. She was fourteen again, too young a creature to hold so many sorrows.

"Say you're sorry, or go," said Yetu, channeling the petulant energy of her recently recalled youth. "I will soon be well enough to clear the boulders on my own. I won't need you to hunt then."

"I am sorry," said Oori, and nothing else.

Yetu nodded. "It's not right to help nurture something back to health, then abandon it before the task is finished. I've come to rely on you," said Yetu. She wasn't used to speaking so freely about her wants and needs. She wasn't used to having wants and needs of her own at all. It had always been a battle between what the wajinru needed, what the ancestors needed, and what she needed. A single lonely girl, her own needs never won.

It was days before Oori and Yetu returned to something approaching their previous level of companionship. Nothing so personal as their earlier discussions, just practical matters. Hunting techniques, currents, winds. Yetu could answer many of Oori's questions about the sea, and Yetu was happy to be her font of knowledge.

"What is the biggest creature in the sea?" asked Oori next, her face stern. Her drive for knowledge wasn't gently curious, as one might expect, but ferocious and consuming. A part of Yetu could understand why she would lust after something like the History so much.

"Leviathan. Like you, she's the last of her kind. Larger than a blue whale by several degrees. She holds air long enough to be underwater for days at a time, and comes up only at night to breathe."

Oori seemed to perk—as much as she ever perked—as she listened.

"She must be lonely," Oori said.

"She's nearly as old as the ocean. It is her companion, as are its many creatures," said Yetu.

"Still. Who could truly know her when there are no others of her kind?" said Oori.

Some days, Oori discussed the place she came from, how there'd been only a few families left for several decades. Disease took all but her in the end. "When there are so few of you, anything can ravage you in moments. What chance did we ever have at survival?" she asked.

Yetu thought she remembered something about another young woman whose family was wiped out in an instant by disease, but she couldn't put it together, couldn't think of who it would be. Another half memory from the rememberings.

"And your husband? Or your wife? Or is it wives? What happened to them?"

Oori snorted. She stood in the water on the other side of the rocks from Yetu, in the shallow part of the open ocean. She had a spear, but she wasn't fishing.

"I have never had any of those things," said Oori.

"Friends?"

"No," Oori said, her voice sad.

"Me neither."

Though that wasn't true, of course. It was a long time ago, so distant now that it seemed to have happened to someone else, but it wasn't someone else. It was Yetu, as a girl, with a small group of peers who tolerated her anxiousnesses. How different might her life have turned out without the History stealing them from her? Would she still love them? Would they have become her lovers or mates? Would they share a den now?

Yetu's gut twisted as she remembered that those girls she once knew were now locked in an eternal state of memory. With no one there to relieve them of its burden, would all of them die? Would they want to kill themselves? Would all the wajinru writhing together turn the ocean into a frothing pit? Would Yetu sink into the hole they created?

The approaching rough weather had all the markings of a wajinru tempest. The slow, slow brew of it, the uncertain and moving center, the feeling of electricity in the air. Yetu had brought this. Her simple but extraordinary rebellion might drown the world if she didn't stop it, *if* she could stop it. Yetu wasn't sure she'd still be able to gather the rememberings from them, the strength of the wajinru en masse too great for her to overcome. She had always struggled to face the darkness, and the thought of returning to the wajinru choked her with dread. The impossible weight of her responsibility to the world would obliterate her before she had the chance to fix what she'd done.

The sky was pale gray with cloud cover. Yetu smelled the coming rain in the air. She'd never experienced such a thing on the surface before, and she was curious what it might be like. She imagined it like gutting an animal. The sky was the belly. Something sharp would come along and slit it open till all its contents spilled out and filled the sea, nourished it.

"You're smiling," said Suka, shaking their head. They didn't come around often, but they occasionally stopped to chat and see how Yetu was doing. "I didn't know that you could do that. What's got you?"

"I'm thinking. I mean, I had a thought. My own thought. My own story." It still pleased her that she could do that, that it was possible to have her mind to herself. Without the History devouring the whole of her mind, she had an inkling of who she was. She didn't have answers yet, but she had questions, endless questions. And worries, and concerns. But they were *hers*.

"What was the thought?"

But Yetu wanted to hold on to it, keep it safe. Who was to say what would happen to it were she to speak it? Suka didn't seem cruel, but Yetu didn't feel sure they wouldn't steal it. They might bring the thought to their people and it would no longer belong to her.

"I haven't had many thoughts of my own. I'd like to keep this one to myself for a while," she said.

Suka nodded companionably. "All right, then, strange fish."

That phrase sparked something, something wonderful and familiar. She wanted to know more, but couldn't.

Yetu turned her gaze out to the water. Sometimes she could see Oori's boat, far out in the distance, the white sail visible, looking like a fin, like a giant creature of the deep itself. A harsh wind blew the sail as rain drizzled. Yetu didn't like it. The patterings against her skin were simultaneously too light and too heavy, and it reminded her of an itch. Water was supposed to exist as a great, singular body.

The tidal pool seemed even smaller now than it had before, and Yetu swam in circles in the shallow, near-pressureless water. It was upsettingly light, warm. She couldn't stretch. She had been here for about three weeks, she guessed. Now that she was mostly recovered, she needed to stretch, to flex.

The boulders separating her from the deeper water were a barrier. Yetu rubbed her front side against it, preparing to slide over. But it still hurt, cartilage twisted and bruised. Even mostly recovered, her body was still a mess of aching bends and joints.

"It hurts in here," Yetu said, cognizant of the water in a way she hadn't been when first swimming to the surface. Her body felt loose, on the verge of falling apart. She might've been built for flexibility, to survive in the deep as well as the shallows, but there was no doubt her body had become accustomed to darkness, to weight, and to density. It did not prefer this thin water. It wanted to be out *there*, where Oori was. Where the wajinru were. She missed them. She missed them more than she'd ever considered possible given that she'd spent the better part of the last two decades shrinking away from them, desperate for solitude. It had only been a few weeks, barely any time at all considering she'd gone a whole year without contact just recently, but this time felt different. It felt like she'd drawn a line and built a wall.

"Can I help you out of there somehow?" Suka asked, a small cloth wrapped around their head and shoulders to stave off the light rain.

"No," said Yetu. She didn't think she was yet strong enough to survive on the other side of the boulders. "I'll heal in time," she said. A few more days rest, that was all Yetu needed, then she could . . . She wasn't sure. She wasn't even sure if she really needed more time, or if fear of the rememberings and by extension the wajinru still haunted her. If she got out of the tidal pool and went back into the ocean, where would she go, and what would she do? Yetu could feel in the water and the sky that the mud womb was broken. She felt it under the brewing weather, a senseless agony bounding outward and sparking the sea. She could no longer convince herself that the wajinru would shake themselves out of the trance, at least not before it was too late.

Yetu should go to them. Now, preferably, healed or not. But something held her here, something murky and louring she couldn't define. Fear of the History played a part, but that wasn't all.

She inhaled sharply through her nose and blew it out through her mouth, the resultant sound whistly and shrill. It was anger. More specifically, resentment. She'd always done what she'd needed to do in service of her people, no matter the cost to herself. To preserve her own life, she'd fled, but now they needed her again, and there she was, willing to sacrifice herself for their benefit.

She'd been denied so much. It was only since escaping, since meeting Oori, that she'd learned what life could be.

Yet emptiness still troubled her. What angered her was the inevitability of it. With the wajinru, she'd been singular and alone. Without them, she'd found Oori and independence, but was cast away from the History and her people. It seemed an impossible choice, and the indecision made her immobile. "Medicine might help heal you faster," said Suka.

Yetu turned to them, so deep in her own thoughts that she'd briefly forgotten that they were there. "You have medicine here?"

Suka nodded. "Of course we do."

"What about venom leaves? They'll help with the swelling and pain."

"Let me ask my sister. She'll know," said Suka. They left, returning not long after with two others, several pouches, and a bowl. "We don't have anything called venom leaves, but we brought a couple of things to try."

"They don't smell appealing," said Yetu.

The two-legs laughed. "No, they don't," said one called Nura. "But you take it, and you'll feel better. Promise. They're powerful pain relievers, and they reduce inflammation and infection, too. Drink. Drink up." Nura pressed the wooden bowl to Yetu's lips and poured it down her throat, droplets of rain dotting Yetu's face.

The scene was so familiar, she could feel herself in Amaba's embrace, taking medicine after her amaba saved her from the sharks.

Yetu choked more of the medicine down, then waved the two-legs away. Like Nura had said, the herbs and tinctures were powerful. A glorious numbness settled over Yetu. She closed her eyes in bliss, then opened them again to stare at the pleasing dark gray of the sky.

With each passing hour, the world darkened yet more.

The ocean smelled bloody. Yetu wanted to dive into it and revel in the coming storm.

She didn't know where she belonged, if returning to the wajinru would mean the death of her. But she wasn't suited for life here.

And where was *here*?

"What do you mean?" asked Oori.

"Where are we? In the world? If you tell me a name, I might know it," Yetu explained.

"Why? What does it matter where any place is, unless you are trying to return to it? It'd do you well not to think of here at all. You're trying to find yourself, aren't you? To do that you must go. Thinking of this place will only hold you back," said Oori.

The storm had arrived and hadn't stopped. It had been raining on and off for two days, and the worst of it was yet to come. Yetu could tell by the look of the waves. She felt . . . She felt a shadow in the water. Even in the little tidal pool. She could liken it only to the vague whiff on her skin she used to get as a child when there was a shark nearby, hungry for her organs.

"I'm trying to get oriented," she said. If she knew where she was in relation to everything else, she could better read the sky and the waves. How big was the land mass they were on? She couldn't get a sense of it locked away in this tiny cage.

"You need to be worrying about out *there*. Not here. You have healed. Only fear keeps you locked in this thing.

What did you tell me before? That you stopped being a historian or whatever it was so you could be free of all that pain. Not so you could waste away your days in a tidal pool," said Oori, who was sitting in the pool bathing herself. She'd started doing that now. In addition to her morning visits, she came after supper to bathe in the tidal pool.

Yetu wasn't sure what the etiquette on these kinds of matters were, but she appreciated seeing more and more of Oori's body. Two-legs covered every part of themselves with clothing, their bodies held in secret from one another. Yetu had wondered at first if it was something like a clam, a defensive casing to protect the soft flesh.

But their clothes were not protective. They were soft. Little more than a bit of woven kelp.

"Stop staring," said Oori.

Yetu looked down at the water. "Apologies," she said. She'd only been curious about the differences between two-legs and wajinru. There were so many. "But may I ask you a question about your body? Well, not yours in particular, but two-legs bodies."

Oori rubbed her body with a mixture of ashes, beef fat, and numerous different flower petals. She scrubbed it all in with a cloth, rubbing till her dark brown skin turned red in places, revealing the blood underneath, the aliveness of her.

"You may ask. But only if I may ask questions of you, too," said Oori.

Yetu's heartbeat quickened when she heard Oori's proposal, but she told herself to remain calm so as not to scare Oori off. Yetu forced her face into a picture of stillness to hide her excitement. How pleasing to think Oori had questions for her just as Yetu had questions for Oori. Oori wanted to know more about Yetu. She believed there was a Yetu to get to know at all.

"Go on, then, before I change my mind," said Oori. "Ask."

Yetu wasn't sure how to phrase her question, as she sensed such topics were taboo among the two-legs based on some conversations she'd had with Suka.

"Come on. Anything," said Oori.

Yetu wiggled her tail fin in the water to take in oxygen, a way of breathing she found more calming than sucking air from the sky through her mouth. "Why is it that some two-legs' genitals hang out such that they are visible through the thin cloth they wear, and why are others' genitals tucked in, only to come out during coupling, I presume?"

Yetu expected Oori to laugh, the way Suka had when Yetu had asked them about breasts. Oori didn't laugh, though. At best, she raised a brow. Bit her lip.

"I'm actually not sure where to start with that," said Oori.

"Is it a choice?" Yetu pressed. Wajinru bodies didn't tend to have differences along those lines, but like two-legs, there were men, women, both, and neither. Such things were self-determined, and Yetu wondered if two-legs had body self-determination too. "You keep yours inside of you. Is that a protective measure, then?"

The cloth Oori used to clean herself had become brown with dead skin and dirt, so she dipped it into the pool to clean it off. When she was done, she worked more of her ash mixture into it and rubbed it over the parts of her body that gave off odor.

"It is not a choice, really. People have different bodies. Different . . . configurations. There is nothing tucked up inside of me. Just a vulva, which is, hmm, a passage that connects—"

"I know what it is," said Yetu. "Does sperm come out of it, then?"

"No," said Oori, unflustered by the questions, which relieved Yetu. Wajinru discussed bodies openly. They were largely if not always naked in front of one another. Through the water, they could feel and hear private things that happened miles away.

Suka, Nura, and the other two-legs on this piece of land seemed less frank about matters. Yetu only knew the precise details of Oori's nakedness because she'd taken to bathing here.

"Does sperm come out of yours?" asked Oori.

Yetu shook her head. "Wajinru have a place to envelope, and then there's something else, and that is what gives sperm. Yet it is always tucked away until the time of mating."

"You have both?" asked Oori.

"Of course."

Oori nodded. "That explains your questions, then. Humans aren't like that. Not everyone is the same.

Not everyone can mate with everyone else and expect a child."

Understanding now, Yetu decided to press further. "When two-legs mate, does it feel good?" she asked, shocked at her own brazenness. Even among wajinru, such questions were considered a personal matter.

"For many," said Oori, as usual, matter-of-fact. Though she showed no signs of continued interest in this conversation, she showed no signs of annoyance either. "For me personally? Only with someone who is quite special in a specific kind of way."

"Someone like who?" asked Yetu.

Oori shook her head. "It is my turn to ask a question."

Smiling, Yetu nodded. "Fair enough. Ask me anything. Please." Perhaps she was too eager. As Oori requested, she wasn't looking at her, but she could smell her and feel the shape of her strange two legs, her split fins, in the water. And the contours of her belly, breasts, and shoulders.

"If wajinru all have such similar parts, how do you choose who does what when you couple?" asked Oori.

Couple was an odd word choice, given it could involve any number of wajinru, frequently up to five, but Yetu didn't inquire further. "What do you mean, who does what?"

"Say you, Yetu, found another wajinru you wanted to be with. Do you . . . untuck?" asked Oori. It was the first time Yetu heard a hint of nervousness and embarrassment in her voice. "Or do you leave it away so that the other may untuck, and . . . you know, insert it into you?"

Heat flooded Yetu's body at Oori's words. She felt dizzy. There was a tugging at the bottom of her belly, a need.

"It is my understanding that it is most common for everything to be . . . engaged at once," said Yetu. "And when not, I suppose it is decided based on the preferences of the wajinru involved in the heat of the moment."

"It is your understanding? Have you not—?"

"I haven't," said Yetu. The urge to avert her gaze overwhelmed her, but it was supplanted by the need to examine every detail of Oori's face. She saw it with her eyes, but she also felt it against her skin, the shape of the passing breeze painting a picture of it on her scaled flesh.

"Would you like to?" asked Oori, sinking deeper into the water. She was scrubbing her hair now, black thick locs, each at least the width of an inch. They were dark like the deep.

"Yes," said Yetu, her voice growing weak and stuttery. "But like you, only with someone special in a particular sort of way." A stranger to these sorts of conversations, she treaded cautiously. It would be too easy to let herself get submerged, to be raptured by the beautiful closeness and say nothing at all, or worse, something foolish.

Oori said nothing, her eyes looking to the sea. She rarely looked Yetu directly in the face. At first, Yetu thought to be offended. Was she really so ugly? So distasteful to the gaze? Yetu often didn't look people directly in the face, and certainly not the eyes, but for Oori it seemed an aversion. Whenever Oori did catch Yetu's gaze, she flitted her eyes away then hardened her face.

Yetu understood now that it was a loneliness. Oori had lost everyone, everything. She couldn't look at another's face and think of anything but the screams of the last remaining specimens of her people.

"And do you find me special in a particular sort of way?" Oori asked, erupting the silence.

Yetu shivered at the note of tenderness in her voice, her throat and mouth uncomfortably dry. She tried to answer, but couldn't speak, instead swallowing a lungful of ocean air, thick with moisture and the scent of salt.

Oori's eyes were still affixed to the sea's horizon, but Yetu caught the faintest flutter of movement as she went to turn toward Yetu then changed her mind, thinking better of it. "I do," answered Yetu finally.

Though she could only see Oori in profile, Yetu saw her cheeks twitch and then plump. She was smiling, and that made Yetu's heart speed up and the pit of her stomach become hot. "And do you find me pleasing to look at?" asked Oori. Just as Yetu's did, Oori's heartbeat quickened with each passing second, causing the water to throb against Yetu's skin.

"Yes. I do," said Yetu, her confidence growing. It felt so good to speak plainly, to know that the answers she gave would be accepted.

"I want you to know that I feel similarly about you," said Oori. Yetu trembled as she tried to steady the flow of water coming in and out of her scales. "But I don't think

I can do this." She stood up then pushed herself up out of the rocks, her naked body fully visible. A consuming desire to be closer to her, to step out of the water even if it killed her, overtook Yetu. She knew not where it came from.

Oori wrapped herself in thick white cloth. "I am going, Yetu."

Yetu nodded, hoping she hadn't revealed too much and frightened Oori away. "I'll see you tomorrow," she said. Despite her resolve to never alter herself for another again, she found herself worrying that she'd said something wrong, something that had made Oori want to go so suddenly. Yetu had asked too many invasive questions, and her answers to Oori's questions had been too frank.

"I won't be back tomorrow," Oori said.

Yetu nodded again, this time less enthusiastically. Oori sometimes went on lengthy boating trips. Maybe it was time to leave the tidal pool. She could follow her. Everything felt so strained still. Her body protested most movement. She'd gotten used to a constant physical gnawing.

"How long will you be gone for, then?" asked Yetu.

"Uncertain. With this storm, I need to take a pilgrimage back to my homeland before it gets worse. I need to protect some of the fixtures, tend to the grave sites, lest they all vanish and the place I'm from become truly dead. I should've gone days ago. Weeks. But I didn't. I wanted to stay. I wanted to stay for you."

Yetu pressed her tail fin into the gushing sand below

to disrupt her breathing. Her chest tightened, and she attempted to keep her body still. "What is a homeland?" Yetu asked, translating it to *home-sea* in her head but unable to make any sense of that.

Oori's face fell, and Yetu searched for all the reasons that might be. Was it a word she was supposed to remember but had forgotten? Had Yetu's question been insensitive in some way? Yetu retraced the conversational steps, the moment Oori's face changed from gently hopeful to a mixture of anger and sadness. She had been expecting Yetu to ask something else. What?

"A homeland is just a place," said Oori, her voice quiet and unsteady. She'd never sounded so defeated. "It's a place that means something because of its history. I know you have a complicated relationship with the past. I do too. But if I don't protect what is left of it there, I will have no homeland. It will just be another place," Oori explained.

Yetu tried to bob her head up and down to nod, but the movement was rigid and forced. "You are leaving me, then?" said Yetu, teeth out, though she hadn't meant them to be. Yetu could only understand a few words Oori had said, too lost in shocked grief to make sense of much more. "Just like that, you are going?" That was the pertinent information. Yetu would be alone again, like she'd been in the deep.

There was Suka. There were other two-legs and surface dwellers. But they did not compare. With Oori, she always wanted more, desperate for time together, for conversation, for closeness. The depth of want seemed endless.

Yetu batted her front fins against the water and made a hard splash, almost soaking Oori's cloth coverings. "Stay. You must stay. Please," she begged, hating herself for it. She'd left the wajinru, seeking out freedom, yet here she was, tethered to another, bending herself toward her. She could not make herself feel nothing for this two-legs, and that was not freedom.

"Come with me," said Oori.

Yetu sunk herself deeper into the sand. She wanted to bury herself alive in it. "I can't. I'm stuck here."

"You and I both know that's not true," Oori said. "Your health is not perfect, but you'll survive, I'll make sure of it. We can protect each other. What is keeping you from the sea? What kind of deep-sea creature prefers a shallow death pit to the infinite ocean?"

What kind of creature, indeed? One who had abandoned the History and the people to whom it belonged. One afraid. One who could neither bear the weight of the rememberings nor the weight of feeling her people suffer through the churning water.

Yetu shook her head. "You're the one who's leaving."

"No, Yetu. You're the one who's not coming with."

Oori had been gone for a day, and the rain had not ceased. Yetu kept her ears open for any sign of where Oori's homeland was, but no one knew. All anyone said about the matter was that the place Oori was from wasn't really a homeland anymore because a homeland needed a people. Without a people, it was just a patch of earth.

That was part of why Oori was going back. This place had meant so much to her, she could not let it become nothing, all traces of it wiped out by storm, a storm Yetu had caused by leaving the wajinru to brood in the rememberings.

Why had she been so stubborn with Oori? Now Oori was on the ocean as the waters grew more and more unsteady. Yetu imagined the brine rising up and filling Oori's throat, imagined the waves upending her craft. She'd let her fear of going back into the ocean stop her from doing what she'd needed to do to keep Oori safe. But Oori wasn't the only one who would suffer. The winds were heavy enough that the trees on the beach shook violently. Branches flew from some of the taller ones onto the sand. The ferocity and the tumult of the sea had increased more than tenfold since Oori had left. Yetu should've known this was coming, how bad it was going to get.

Suka had come to visit her to see how she was doing. Yetu had yelled at them to go inland and to take as many people as they could with them. They weren't new to storms, but they'd likely not seen anything like what was coming. An echo of a remembering reverberated through Yetu. The same images she'd seen when she first came here washed over her afresh. Drowning two-legs. War between the wajinru and the surface dwellers. In such a battle, the two-legs would surely lose, for what being on this earth could compete with the might of the ocean? Suka and their family might die, and it would be Yetu's fault. She'd have to live with that for the rest of her days. Her bid to save herself, to save her life, would have the unintended consequence of killing others.

Oori would die too. Eventually, so would the wajinru; for if they had not found their way out of the trance of remembering by now, it didn't seem likely to happen. They were so lost in it, they were taking their grief out on the whole world.

Then there would just be Yetu, all alone. There would be quiet. The waters would settle. The winds would slow. The rememberings would perish with the wajinru. The wajinru would have the same fate as Oori's people. Much of the world would.

Storm waters filled the tidal pool, dark and murky, blotting out Yetu's view of the teeming life inside. The future, too, was dark, if there was a future at all. The hurt that coursed through Yetu as she imagined a future-less world rivaled the pain of the rememberings. Could it really be that there was a version of the world where everything would be eradicated? Gone? She imagined how it felt when the History left her, the freedom of it, but if freedom only brought loneliness, emptiness, what was the point?

Nothingness was a fate worse than pain. How long would it take for Yetu to become ravenous for something to fill the hole the way other wajinru did? She doubted she could last even a year. She was already aching to see Oori, but also her amaba.

At least with pain there was life, a chance at change and redemption. The rememberings might still kill her, but the wajinru would go on, and so, too, would the rest of the world. The turbulent waves were a chaos of her own making, and it was time to face them.

8

How long has it been "tonight"? Lost in the endless madness of the Remembrance, we all starve, unable to nurture our bodies. Our bodies wane but our minds swell with pains too large to contain. Such imbalances cannot last.

Foolish Zoti, to think there is ever a way to guard against harm, to protect prosperity. Everything ends. How she would cry to know what became of her legacy.

We wajinru live Zoti's ignorant lie for centuries, convinced our castles in the deep can shield us. The ocean is more than our home or birthplace. It is our heaven, too. For we were knit together by the powers of its life force. When we die, it is where we remain. Therefore we nurture it as it has nurtured us. We bring life to it as it brought life to us.

This is our covenant, maintained for years, until we are Basha.

In the old days, when we discovered a ship that threw our ancestors into the sea like refuse, we sunk it. Now we will sink the world.

There is chatter about dead children.

"Is there anything about this in the History?" Omju asks. "Something that can tell us how to proceed?"

Someone else asks, "Basha?"

"Historian Basha! Honored one!"

We hear them call us, our name ringing out through the water, but we are too entranced in a remembering to respond, one made by the third historian. The History troubled her so deeply that she did not believe it. She thought it was a trick of the ancestors, a test she had to pass. The third historian wondered if a woman called Zoti really had seen bodies cast overboard into the sea, left to drown.

When she went upward to see if it was true, she was snagged by a hook and lifted onto a boat deck. She tried to heave in oxygen through her mouth and nose, but she didn't know how. Suffocating, she half passed out. The two-legs (they were real!) tried to grab and handle her, but she was more awake than they thought, and she bit every one of their throats until they died. She flopped and crawled to the boat edge, using her front fins to pull herself forward. With one powerful but painful thwack of her tail fin, she was back into the sea, having cleared the short wall.

She did not see the supposed surface dwellers who

abandoned bodies of their own kind like an emptied-out clamshell, but she had no trouble believing the two-legs were capable of it after seeing them in the flesh.

This truth, that two-legs were cruel and unusual, was the most important lesson of the History, and the third historian vowed to protect her people from them.

"Basha!"

We awake from the remembering as they call our name, head aching and body overly alert, overly sensitive.

"We need your great knowledge, Basha," said Omju.

We don't care for Omju at all, who always comes to us with his silly questions, but is also always so certain of his way. He presents himself as knowledgeable, as the keeper of traditions. He is the closest person wajinru have to a leader or queen. His made-up council agrees with whatever he wants.

We do not answer his questions. We barely acknowledge that he is speaking to us at all. Mostly we do this because it makes him reconsider his self-importance. Smiling, we turn and swim toward—something.

Restless energy builds up in us, wanting to explode. Our amaba used to call this spoiling for a fight. And it's true, we always were, always still are. We don't know what to do with quietness, with peace. Life in the deep has never suited us.

Amaba says we came out gnawing and biting. Chewed our own cord away. But it never filled us. We never wanted milk. Only meat.

We didn't get along with others, finding their

conversations slow and inane. Our mind moved so quickly while the world passed by slowly.

When we found out we'd be taking on the History, we were glad. For once, there was something that could keep up with our racing thoughts. When the previous historian transferred the rememberings to us, we sparked alive with the feel of the past rushing into us, making sure no part of us was ever empty again.

Where the History saddened others, we felt only a glorious, burning anger. We liked the challenge of it. It suited us. Anger was our favorite emotion. We were at home in it. It gave us purpose.

As we swim into the dark city, we attune ourselves to the chatterings of others. They want to know what could've caused such a thing, the deaths of a small group of wajinru children. We feel fears and anxieties rustle against our skin. Their confusion skims our scales. What mighty beast could bring down three wajinru children so deep in the ocean? We are the apex predators of the entire sea.

Clueless wajinru gossip as they wander the waters. They would know the answer to this question if they lived beyond the bubble of wajinru cities, if they listened to the things we had to say more than just when it was convenient. We cannot understand a people that would willingly choose to cut itself off from its history, no matter what pain it entails. Pain is energy. It lights us. This is the most basic premise of our life. Hunger makes us eat. Tiredness causes us to sleep. Pain makes us avenge.

We are not wajinru if being wajinru means distancing ourselves from pain. We embrace pain, seek it out.

We make a path through the water, people splitting their parties to accommodate us. They fear us. This reaction doesn't bother us. We aren't to be trifled with. It is good that they recognize this.

After several strokes, we see a muted orange light. It's Ephras holding a bioluminescent *cretuk*, and we swim toward him. An explosion had burned Ephras badly enough that he has difficulty feeling around anymore. What happened to him was the same thing that had happened to the children, though he'd been spared death. Still, he needs the aid of the light to properly see without being able to sense words and objects against his skin.

"You came," says Ephras.

"Of course."

Ephras gestures for us to follow him, then begins swimming toward his den a mile outside the city. He has to move slowly and carefully, unable to navigate without the aid of the light.

"I thought perhaps the council might be holding you up, keeping you away," says Ephras.

"The council has no hold over me," we say.

"You should pretend to tolerate them more. You don't want them as enemies," says Ephras, but it isn't really advice, more a general observation.

"If they ever decide to make themselves into a problem, I'll address it at that time. Until then, I won't worry about it," we say, happy to follow Ephras wherever he leads us. He is the only living thing in the world for whom that statement is true.

The water grows quieter and stiller as we move toward the outskirts of the city. We don't like the silence, the emptiness. Except now, when it is with him.

"You don't worry about anything," says Ephras, "save that you secretly worry about everything." He shakes his head then twists his body into a sequence of elaborate spirals. We watch him intently, thrilled by the wild beauty of it. There are others not far from us; otherwise we would swim more closely to him so that our bodies were touching, grazing against each other as we pulsed forward in the water.

Generally, historians are not to take lovers. It is seen as a distraction from the sacred task of protecting the History. We have no interest in laws or customs. The wajinru are in no position to tell us what to do. They'd do well not to ask anything of us and be grateful for what we occasionally choose to give them.

When we arrive at Ephras's den, we embrace him, our bodies curling together. No one else can pull tenderness from us like this, make us weak with longing. It is a weakness we cherish.

Before him, it was only anger that could bring us to a tremble. Ephras showed us there are other ways to live on the brink.

We mate until we are spent.

"So," Ephras says.

"Don't."

"You need to tell them who's behind this," says Ephras.

"They won't listen," we argue.

"Make them listen. The council has explicitly come to you for help. I would say they're ready to hear what you have to say."

It's an illusion of open dialogue. They want an easy answer. A quick trick to fix the problem of the recent attacks upon us. They want me to tell them it's some barely known underwater creature, and if we just do this, we can beat it.

But these explosions, these strange hot-fire beasts who take us by surprise, they reek of the two-legs. Two-legs don't live in the deep and therefore can't be fought in the deep, not with the weapons they obviously have.

"Children are dead," Ephras says, leaving our embrace.

We nod. "And more will die. Perhaps even most of us. But they will not do what's necessary to prevent that."

"Then convince them to do it. Or convince others and we can do it without the council. People believe in you."

"They fear me," we say.

"Wajinru will do what you say, regardless of the council's recommendation," Ephras says.

We circle Ephras's den. Can't stay still. Claustrophobic, we swim out into the sea, where the water is much colder.

Ephras comes after us, but he's forgotten his *cretuk* lantern and stumbles into us clumsily. We grab hold to steady him, our fins on his shoulders. We feel every nook and cranny of him as the sensation of his body moving in the water sends waves against our skin. We rest our head on his shoulder.

"Basha. Please. I don't want to die, and I could not bear it if you died. Or my amaba, or any of my pod. My siblings. I have never seen or felt anything like that—what did you call it?—bomb, in my entire life. We are not ready. We must prepare. We must do something. I've never been this scared of anything."

He weeps as we hold each other with our front fins. We will ourselves not to be bent by his words, but truthfully, we would die for him. And we will always do anything he asks of us.

Omju and the council do not listen, but other wajinru do.

We go to the sacred waters and wait. When we are here, people come. We need not even call them. The sense memory of the Remembrances is strong enough in them that the slightest tweak in the water alerts them of our presence even miles and miles away.

When Omju arrives, he calls this gathering unauthorized. "Unauthorized by whom?" we ask.

"Me!" says Omju.

"And who are you?" we ask.

We shoo him away as he tries to answer. The sacred waters fill with wajinru despite his claims. People are worried about the recent deaths and know instinctively that a new world is coming. They believe we will have answers where the council doesn't.

"Wajinru," we begin, addressing the masses gathered

around. Perhaps twenty-five thousand. Perhaps more. "Seventy-five years ago, under the time of the previous historian, beings from above came down into our waters caged in metal fish to scout what lay beneath here. They came multiple times, but claimed only one life. An older wajinru woman who was caught up in the metal fish's spinning back fin. She died in such agony that the historian felt it, swimming toward her to capture her memories in time."

They gasp as we speak.

"It cut her up into pieces. In the rememberings, I have been her as she died. I know intimately what it feels like to be spun by blades to death. But as I tell you this, the most important thing to know is: This is not even a speck of what the two-legs are capable of."

"Two-legs?" several call out.

"They are surface dwellers. They do not live in the sea, but on the land, and they walk on fins that split all the way up to their thighs, called legs," we say, leaving out other details that they're likely not ready for.

"Those who came before were scouters. Their purpose was to see what gifts of the deep they could steal from us. Below us, deep beneath the sand, there is a substance they crave. It is their life force. Their food. They feast on it like blood."

The crowd of wajinru shudder at that imagery. "What is it? What is this thing?"

"I know not its name. Only that we are rich with it, and they would mine it from us like scavenger creatures picking off bones," we say. "For whatever reason, they left us in peace for some time, but they are back now, with weapons. They have spent the intervening years honing their special tools. What they did then was beyond what any of us can understand. Think what they can do now."

The sacred waters are not holy and silent after we speak. It sounds like the bustling city. Constant movement, constant conversation. "Then what do we do?" someone asks.

We have been waiting our whole lives for someone to ask such a question. "We fight."

The council wields more power over wajinru than Ephras said. They convince them we are simply dramatic, so maddened by the rememberings that we make up lies.

"A metal fish with a spinning tail fin with land dwellers inside?" Omju says. "It is something only a foolhardy, stubborn man like Basha could make up. He wants a war because he was born for battle. Do not listen to him."

Ephras holds us tight as Omju makes the announcement that the wajinru will not be fighting. They will set up perimeters to protect our waters, but nothing more, because anything else would be excessive, would be entertaining the fantasies of a madman hungry for blood.

We are hungry for blood, that is not untrue. We may well be mad, too. We swim and swim until a remembering takes us to Zoti, the moment she saw a living two-legs thrown overboard. We come out of the memory angrier than we were before. We cannot settle.

For days we swim and swim without cease, without rest. We only pause to eat, and we purposefully seek out big, challenging prey. We know that Ephras is worried for us, especially with little means to find us.

It's the sound of death that finally draws us back home. There's a thunderous roar that near deafens us. It stuns our scales and we cannot orient ourselves. We spin in a dizzy loop for ages, passing out then waking again. Screams call us from the distance. The deep smells like burnt things.

When we make it back to the city, we pay no mind to the carnage. We are only looking for Ephras. At least his body. Please let there still be a body. We need to hold it one last time.

After that we will find Omju, if he is not dead already, and devour him.

"Basha!"

Ephras is alive. He is well, sustaining no injuries but the one from his previous encounter. Hundreds of others are not so lucky. We fume. Not even Ephras can calm us, and soon we are shooting sparks of electricity through the water, stirring it up with our rage. We want to fight, but as hungry as we are for battle, we know it would be foolish to proceed alone.

We consider abandoning reason when more die, as our restraint is nearly overwhelmed by the desire to fight back. Another batch of a hundred die in a blink. Then thrice that much in an assault on a small village on the seafloor. We wait to be numbed by it, for the grief to become so much that we no longer feel it. That point never arrives. Our numbers reduce, and the rage grows.

We know we need to fight, but how? We have been humbled.

It is not long before our sprawling city is gone. All traces of dwellings, ash. Omju says we need to go outward, to expand to other sections of the deep and build there. We tell him what's really necessary is to go upward.

"We must go to them. Fight them. The ocean made us. Therefore it will take care of us," we say. "We must simply call on it."

Omju tries to interrupt us, and we hurl our body toward his, signaling a fight. "If you want to be king of the wajinru so badly, then be willing to fight for it. Be willing to fight *me* for it," we say.

Not one to further sacrifice his reputation to the onlookers already disappointed in him, Omju shows his teeth. Like us, he is small and agile, but we have the benefit of generations of wajinru fighters and warriors. We know everything they know. We've learned all they've learned.

We go for his throat, and he is done, his breathing apparatus inside our own.

"There has been a change in regime," we say. There will be no more foolish leaders. No more councils. We are the historian. We carry the sacred rememberings. Who but us knows enough to lead?

The wajinru are no longer frightened of us. They are

emboldened by what we represent: war with the creatures who cut our population in half. "The two-legs will not stop until we are extinct," we say. "Like salmon, like the mighty hammerhead, monk seals, various sea turtles, fin whales, and so many others. Are you ready to take back what belongs to us?"

Amassed in a single unit, a chorus, we swim upward. The warmth from the sun-touched waters weakens us, and we rest for days before ascending higher.

We pass on rememberings to them. They must have the depravity of the two-legs fresh in their minds. Ephras swims next to us. He is never out of our line of sight.

Many cannot survive the rush of light and heat. Is the sun any different than the bombs? With all the pain so fresh, many choose simply to sink and die. The others we stir to action with more memories. Psychically linked, we are stronger. Our connection makes us a beast mightier than the blue whale.

We swim upward and upward, bodies in formation. We are arranged in rings, a circle of forty over a circle of forty over a circle of forty and so on. We move in a spiral as we ascend, creating a twister in the water.

Not all of us survive. For some, the shock of the near pressureless water compared to the deep is too much, and they die. Two-legs wage war against us, even as we've left the place they want so badly to claim as their own. They know we're coming for them.

The power of our upward motion agitates the water into a protective cyclone only wajinru can enter. Our shared fury makes us stronger. We continue to rise.

As we near the surface, we lose sight of what we are doing. We are not Basha anymore. It is like we are in every remembering at once. We are every wajinru. As one, we make the ocean waters rise and create a tidal wave that lifts us high above land.

This is the first time the other wajinru are seeing the two-legs outside of the Remembrance. They are shocked by their faces, similar in many ways to our own. They know what we have known since taking on the History. The two-legs are our kin.

This does not make us more gentle. It has the opposite effect. We send endless waves of salt water onto the land, flooding the whole earth. This is only our first assault.

We remember.

9

Rain fell with such force that Yetu half convinced herself that the sky was another ocean. Since Suka's departure, the precipitation had increased from a steady pulsing to a smothering. Were the surface dwellers to look up, they'd drown.

Yetu worried for Oori and the other surface dwellers, who were likely unprepared for this wrath from the heavens. She worried for her fellow wajinru, too, suffering woefully because of her neglect of duty.

No easy solution presented itself to her, no scenario where Yetu maintained her peace and freedom, and the world survived.

Maybe the sacrifice of a single person was the only path forward. It would result in the fewest amount of deaths. Yetu knew how to contain the rememberings. If she took them back, the uproar in the water causing this storm would calm, saving two-legs lives, including Suka, their people, and Oori. It would save the wajinru from their grief. Yetu hoped that they hadn't already starved themselves.

The sea rose as rainwater bashed its surface. Waves crashed over the boulders surrounding the tidal pool. Yetu sunk down into it. She couldn't jump the rocks with so little room to give herself proper leverage, but she could still gather up her strength. She let the salt water cleanse her with its mix of constancy and fluidity. A beautiful reminder of balance.

Yetu tuned in to that essence as she let herself be buried by ocean in the small pool. The burn of salt and the cool flow of water. The warmth she'd felt for Oori and the sadness that had flooded her when she'd chosen to leave. Wanting to see her amaba alive again. Wanting the world to exist, to be more than just a place with a history no one would ever know.

These didn't have to be contradictions. She let the multiple truths exist inside her as a way of meditating. It was something that she'd learned to do when dealing with the rememberings, to try to find a modicum of quiet and accept the multitudes inside herself. She never reached calm, nor even a steadiness, but she did it anyway. It made her remember that she existed.

She luxuriated in the sloshing water. Tiny fish fluttered past her again, reminding her that she was alive. A crab clicked against the stones above, far from shelter. Water, outside her in the pool, inside her body in the form of life-sustaining blood and wet tissue, both connected. She saw it all move in a circle as real as a remembering. Inside her, outside her, one.

As she felt herself carried away in the rush of feeling, her body seemed to ignite, electric. She'd never felt so synchronized with the ocean before. Her emotions were as dark and tumultuous as the deep. Spurred by her need to leave and leave now, she zeroed in on the water with as much focus as she could, hoping this would work.

"Rise!" Yetu said. If she could generate enough charge in her body, the water would be attracted to her, and she could bend it.

"Rise!" she said again, not to the water, but to herself, demanding her body to focus. "*Rise.*"

The water moved, but not to her will. Storm and wind jostled it, but she could feel that more was possible, as emotions and sensations kindled her body into sharp awareness. If the wajinru could bring this tempest, she could make the water in the tidal pool carry her to freedom.

Yetu closed her eyes and stopped breathing with her mouth. She visualized the water in the tidal pool going upward to great heights, carrying her over the boulder back to the sea.

There was a stir in the pool, distinct from its normal movement. Yetu reached out to it using the same technique she did when she reached out to the wajinru during the Remembrance. She had to slit herself open and spill herself out. Yetu gave her whole being to the ocean the way the ocean had given all of itself to her, giving the wajinru the spark of life, showing them that if only they knew how, water could be breathed.

With that, the water rose, and Yetu cleared the rocks. As soon as she splashed back into the open sea, she swam toward the center of the coming hurricane, ignoring the pain that still touched every part of her.

The deep embraced her, and oh, how glorious the dark was. Her eyes had been burning for weeks, and she hadn't realized until the open ocean soothed the ache. Racing as fast as she could, she made it to the wajinru in only three hours. The wajinru were still in the sacred waters, though their flailing had destroyed the thick walls of the womb. Despite the wajinru being cradled in the ocean's depths, their turmoil had affected the whole sea, extending up to the surface where the storm raged.

Yetu watched them with her ears and skin. Their bodies seized in a thousand different directions. Though individuals quaked to the rhythms of their own bodies, as a whole they moved as one. Together they formed a giant teardrop, but there was no pattern to any single wajinru's movement.

The wajinru were thin and malnourished. While Yetu had been onshore feasting on Oori's offerings, they'd lost the ability to hunt, too deep in the trance. Three weeks without food had shrunken their bodies.

Yetu swam closer. It wouldn't work to shout. Shouting had never woken Yetu from being lost in the History.

Instead she channeled her energy into connecting with them, the same way she would've done traditionally at the end of a Remembrance before taking the History back. She touched each one of them, figuring out who each wajinru was outside of the oneness the Remembrance brought.

That mattered. Who each of them was mattered as much as who all of them were together. For so long, the wajinru hadn't felt like living creatures to Yetu. Just a mass that fed off her rememberings for their own benefit. But like Yetu, they were their own people too. They'd not asked for the emptiness any more than Yetu had asked for the History.

Amaba had said it herself before the Remembrance: they were cavities. Oori had felt that way too, robbed of her people's past.

It shouldn't be that way, and it wouldn't have to. Yetu would search every last remembering of the History until she found a way to free her people from this cursed relationship of wajinru to historian, but first she needed to take the rememberings back on.

The water was ripe with electrical energy, and it took her no time at all catch their flow. Their minds plowed hers, knocking her over physically so that she rushed backward in the water.

Desperate, they clawed at her for mental purchase, and Yetu let them. It was like a thousand sets of teeth were biting into her at once, but she relaxed into it. She had to do this: for her amaba and the rest of the wajinru,

145

for Suka and their family, and for Oori, whose homeland was likely already destroyed.

Yetu let her people flow into her, then focused on their thoughts. The rememberings were happening all at once. Millions of memories. Without time.

Yetu recognized each one. A part of her had held on to this, or it had held on to her. She plucked rememberings one by one. With time and distance, their impact had become less visceral, less gutting. She wept as her people wept, but she was able to maintain her focus.

"Yetu!" someone called.

Overwhelmed by the effort necessary to relieve the wajinru of the History, she didn't recognize the voice at first.

"My Yetu."

It was Amaba. She'd found her child through the haze of rememberings. "Stop. Stop."

The voice grew louder. Amaba was coming closer. Yetu couldn't imagine how she was navigating the waters with all that was happening.

"I will save you," Yetu said.

"You will not," shouted Amaba. "Stop!"

Yetu kept plucking rememberings, reabsorbing them into herself. She needed to concentrate, or the accumulation of agonies would undo her.

Then Amaba was on her, holding her tight. "Stop this! Stop!"

Yetu jerked away. She was desperate to prevent the future without the wajinru, without Oori, without any history at all. Even if she was not successful in saving the world, she could save the memories of it. Pain filled her, but so did knowledge, beauty. She felt mighty Basha's fury turn to softness when in the embrace of his lover. She felt Zoti's longing for companionship and how it had given her the ambition to make the wajinru into a people, a chorus. All of these things had made Yetu.

It wasn't all pretty, but it was hers. If it was a choice between the History and emptiness, maybe Yetu wanted the History. She'd always complained that the rememberings erased her, that Yetu didn't exist because the ancestors took up too much space inside her. That was all still true, but what did it matter whether she existed if she was alone, if all that was around her was abyss?

"Please! There must be another way," said Amaba. She spoke in the rudimentary language of electric charges. "You don't have to live with this pain alone. Join us."

Yetu ignored her amaba, absorbing more memories. She had thrown away her ancestors.

"You didn't throw them away. You lived. You did what you needed to do to make sure you lived. Our survival honors ancestors more than any tradition," said Amaba. Her fins were pressed against Yetu's cheeks. Her face looked hollow, but her dark eyes were vibrant.

Yetu felt the minds of every living wajinru. Their struggles were so familiar to her. "Join us," said Amaba, begging. "I would sooner die than let you suffer this alone. You begged me to understand, and I never did. I never could. Now I know, my child. I know, and I will not see you bear it without your amaba, without your kindred."

But maybe she didn't have to. Maybe, instead of taking the History from them, she could join them as they experienced it. Just like with the Remembrance, she could guide them through the rememberings so it didn't overtake them with such violence. They could bear it all together.

Usually, after the Remembrance, the historian waited nearby, empty of memories, but what would happen if they stayed? What could happen if someone with experience stayed with the wajinru past the moment of completion? Could she wrangle them back toward consciousness, without taking the memories back? Could they live out their days all sharing the memories together?

Zoti Aleyu wanted the wajinru to be one, together. But they never were. They were two. Historian and her subjects. It was time for the two to be merged.

Yetu let herself feel how the other wajinru felt, flooded by sensation. She welcomed the barrage of thoughts. They subsumed her, the same way they subsumed everyone else.

"I am here," she said. "Enough."

"It hurts," they cried. "We hurt."

"Yes," said Yetu, acknowledging their pain in a way it never had been for her.

Yetu ebbed and flowed with them, caught up in the wave of rememberings, but she'd learned over the years how to make an inch for herself.

"How?" someone asked, and it came out as all of them asking it in unison. "How do we make an inch?"

Yetu showed them a picture of the day with the sharks, how lost she'd been, bleeding, seconds away from death before her amaba scooped her up and dragged her to safety. "We must save one another," said Yetu.

Yetu showed them what she did when she found the History most overwhelming and brutal, projecting images from her own mind into theirs. When the History threatened to end Yetu, she went to one memory in particular: their first caretaker. In this remembering, there is a lone wajinru pup floating, alive and content. It was the ocean who was their first amaba.

It took three days for the storm inside all of them to settle. They each held pieces of the History now, divvied up between them. They shared it and discussed it. They grieved. Sometimes, they wanted to die. But then they would remember, it was done.

Whenever an event triggered a remembering, they spoke those words. "It is done." Because it was. Yetu thought of life on the surface for Oori. She had lost most things. Knowledge, rituals, prayers, family. Gaps could be survived and made full again, but only if you were still living.

"You look woeful," said Amaba.

"I am trying to remember something," Yetu said.

"What?" her amaba asked.

"What it was like to be in the womb."

She'd always thought the first memory had been the stranded wajinru pups, tethered to their dead first mothers, but if wajinru existed before the birth, inside the bellies, there should be memories of that, too.

Yetu explained her thought to Amaba.

"It is possible you have had a remembering of such a thing, but have forgotten it."

It was impossible to forget. "What do you mean?"

"Do you have memories of darkness?" asked Amaba.

"Of course."

"Of loneliness?"

"Yes."

"All I'm saying," said Amaba, "is that there is very little difference between a bornt wajinru pup and one still encased in the womb. What if some of your rememberings of dark loneliness as a pup were you inside a belly, and it was hardly distinguishable from floating in the deep? It is all waters."

Yetu circled her mother slowly. "It is all waters."

"When I think about the rememberings I've had, I believe this to be the case. I remember the womb from the first wajinru. I remember the ocean teaching us to breathe water. Once we were born, it would've been too late, but in the womb, it came to us naturally. That is why it changed us then."

It was strange to be having such a conversation with her amaba, discussing their varied interpretations of the History. What had always seemed certain to Yetu wasn't so immutable. The living put their own mark on the dead.

Goodness, how had she missed it?

"I need to look for someone," admitted Yetu. "She

is probably dead, but regardless, I would like to at least locate her body. She means a great deal to me."

"Oh? A wajinru?"

"A two-legs."

Amaba tried to act neutral but Yetu caught her attempt to smooth down a smile into cold neutrality. "She had markings on her face, these beautiful, intricate tattoos. Some of the symbols were identical to etchings on the comb I received shortly before the last Remembrance. One of the offerings made to me. I'd assumed they were bite marks, but of course, they are not. They were intentional carvings. I misinterpreted."

"It is easy to do that with the past, even with the blessing of the full visions of the History," said Amaba.

Yetu showed Amaba the comb. "My Oori comes from the place where this object is from. Does it spark anything for you? A location?"

Amaba held the comb in her front fin and rubbed it with closed eyes. "It's from a song."

"What?" asked Yetu.

"A song our amaba used to sing when she was pregnant." Yetu understood that when Amaba said *our amaba*, she was speaking in the voice of the Remembrance, when everybody became one.

"You remember such things?" asked Yetu.

Amaba began to sing. "Zoti aleyu, zoti aleyu, watsa tibi m'besha tusa keyu?"

Strange fish, strange fish, why do you jump around in my belly like a fish out of water?

Yetu had heard the song before. She'd just dismissed it as an old conversation with her amaba, something from her own childhood.

She'd taken on the History so young that memories from the past blended with memories of her life. Amaba was old enough that her memories were more distinct.

"I know where she is," Yetu said, and left her amaba at once to try to find Oori.

Waj, the first surface dweller a wajinru had befriended, had lived on an island called Tosha. It was the wajinru word for *belonging*. It was also the Tosha word for *belonging*.

Waj had told Zoti, the first historian, where she was from, where she was heading. Zoti had misinterpreted. Perhaps Waj had deliberately played with her.

It was a small island in the backward C-shaped cradle of the African continent, and it took Yetu a day to swim there. She didn't know if Oori would even still be there. It had been a while now since the storm had passed.

Yetu swam close to the shore, careful not to beach herself. "Oori!" she screamed, her voice ugly, strange, and coarse. "Oori!"

She called her nonstop for hours, her voice as loud as she could manage. Finally, she gave up, accepting reality. If Oori was here, she was not coming.

Yetu waited days, eyes on the tree line, waiting for Oori to emerge. She did not. Yetu neither ate nor slept. She certainly didn't leave. A world where a storm she had made killed the two-legs she held so dear was not bearable. Yetu remembered Zoti and Waj, but it was not the same. Oori had asked Yetu to come with her, and Yetu had willingly denied her. She'd never forgive herself.

On the seventh day, Yetu turned back to the open sea, where she saw a sail on the horizon. She squinted, the sun a blight against her eyes. Dazed from lack of food and rest, she wasn't sure that she wasn't sleeping. "Oori," she said quietly, her voice ravaged from the days she'd spent shouting for her. "Please, please, please," she begged, her heartbeat quickening.

The boat was coming in fast, the winds strong.

When Oori saw Yetu, she did not wave happily, but she did lower her sail so as not to run Yetu over. It was perhaps the closest she'd ever get to a gesture of love.

Then Oori jumped into the water next to Yetu. Her small boat was not anchored and drifted away quickly on the waves.

"Your boat," said Yetu.

"Hopefully the tide will carry it in. Or it won't."

"I have longed for you since you left," said Yetu. "Were you able to get here in time?"

"No," said Oori. Neither of them said anything for several moments until Oori added quietly but steadily, "I longed for you, too." Then she began to cry like she'd been holding it in her whole life. Yetu thought she probably had. Oori had been waiting for someone to bear witness. "I thought I'd never see you again. I thought— I thought what happened to my family, to my nation. I thought that had happened to you."

"I'm here," said Yetu. "I will stay with you no matter what."

"It's all gone. All of it," she said.

Yetu nodded. "All but for you," she said, shivering at the feel of Oori's legs treading water. "And this." Yetu showed Oori the comb.

Oori studied it with sharp, serious eyes, her brow pinched tightly together as she bit her lower lip. "Where did you get this?"

"It is from one of the first mothers. The wajinru's earliest ancestors."

Oori blinked several times as she processed and wept silently. "When I die, there will be none of us left."

"Then don't die," Yetu said.

A bare shadow of a smile pressed through Oori's usual glum countenance.

"Stay with me, and we will make a new thing. What's behind us, it is done."

"How could I possibly stay with you?"

"Didn't you know the ocean grants wishes?" asked Yetu.

It wasn't really that simple. Of course, Yetu didn't believe that the sea was sentient. But it was where life began. It was where the life of the wajinru began, and reaching backward, the life of the two-legs, too.

"Let me show you something?" asked Yetu.

Oori tried to wipe the tears from her face, but her hands were wet from the water, and finally that was when she laughed, at her own silliness. "Show me anything, everything," she said, swimming closer so that her thighs brushed against Yetu as her legs moved furiously to keep herself afloat.

"It might be easier if we touch."

"Touch me, then," said Oori.

They held each other close until Yetu was able to transfer to Oori the remembering of the womb. Lost in it, Oori stopped treading, and she sank a little. Yetu let her sink, holding her tightly so she could quickly return her to the surface if need be.

But when Oori jolted from the remembering, she was breathing underwater, just as she'd breathed in the womb.

She did not transform in the way wajinru pups transformed in the two-legs' bellies. She didn't grow gills or fins, but like Yetu, she could breathe both on land and in the sea. She was a completely new thing.

Yetu beckoned her downward into the dark, into this world of beauty. For most of her life, Yetu had had to shut it out, split between the past and the present, her mind unable to manage even the dullest input. But the world was infinite and magnificent, and she had finally found her place in it.

"Come," said Yetu. Oori followed. This time, the two-legs venturing into the depths had not been abandoned to the sea, but invited into it.

AFTERWORD
by clipping.

THE BOOK YOU CURRENTLY HOLD IN YOUR HANDS—
and are likely upset that you read too quickly and that is
now over—is only one step in what its editor, Navah Wolfe,
described as a game of artistic Telephone. You know how
the game works: A phrase is whispered from ear to ear, and
as it's misheard by each participant, the cumulative errors
transform the phrase into something new and unexpected.
It's an obvious metaphor, and something of a cliché, but
it's usually deployed to illustrate how signal accumulates
noise, how transduction degrades information, how truth
becomes fiction when it's passed along as gossip. What
that use of the metaphor ignores is that the phrase's transformation is a *feature* of Telephone, not its failure—it's
what makes the game fun. Each new telling of *The Deep*
has been productive, rather than destructive, and each
new iteration has been carried out with admiration for the

previous. *The Deep* has gone through three major rounds of Telephone to find itself now in book form, and might continue indefinitely, happily taking on the adaptations of each new interpreter, into the future.

Drexciya started the game. The Detroit techno-electro duo of James Stinson and Gerald Donald—along with collaborators like "Mad" Mike Banks and Cornelius Harris of Underground Resistance, illustrators like Frankie Fultz and Abdul Qadim Haqq, DJ Stingray, members of the Aquanauts, and others—created the original mythology:

> Could it be possible for humans to breathe underwater? A foetus in its mother's womb is certainly alive in an aquatic environment. During the greatest holocaust the world has ever known, pregnant America-bound African slaves were thrown overboard by the thousands during labor for being sick and disruptive cargo. Is it possible that they could have given birth at sea to babies that never needed air? Are Drexciyans water-breathing, aquatically mutated descendants of those unfortunate victims of human greed? Have they been spared by God to teach us or terrorize us?

Their story took one of the most gruesome details of the Atlantic slave trade and reframed it. The murder of enslaved women was reimagined as an escape from murderous oppression, and the founding of a utopian civilization. Drexciya's music was, for the most part, instrumental, and what lyrics there were provided only small glimpses into the mythology they had created. As writer Kodwo Eshun explains: "It was a world that was only being filled in partially, track by track, and you were doing a lot of that navigating, with the help of the music and the track titles. In a sense, to be a Drexciya fan was to build the mythos by yourself." With our song "The Deep," we took up that project, navigating the undersea world that Stinson and Donald had created, filling in and building upon that mythos for ourselves.

Drexciya's music has fascinated us, ever since we encountered it many years ago, for several reasons. For one thing, we admired how much story they were able to tell with so little written content. With a combination of only several hundred words, they created a fictional universe that nonetheless felt real to us. In our music we have always been focused on storytelling. We often talk about lyrics and themes as if we were writing short stories or novels. Although *Splendor & Misery*—the 2016 science-fiction concept album we made before we made "The Deep"—contains considerably more words than appeared in Drexciya's entire oeuvre, we often referred to their technique of spare, elliptical world-building when we were making it. We wanted listeners to fill in the narrative and cocreate the world of the album as they heard it.

In the second place, we admired the fact that Drexciya's elaborate, ambitious concepts were grounded in the most functional of music. Their tracks serve at least one concrete purpose above all: they make you dance. And this is not to say that they bridge some sort of highbrow/ lowbrow divide—because we don't believe in such a thing—but it's essential to remember that Drexciya were much more than their narrative themes. To this day, the experience of listening to their music is communal, and it is deeply physical. This is as much a part of their politics as was the science-fiction story of Drexciya—the rave, the block party, the live concert . . . they are all approaches to utopian world-building. Drexciya continue to teach us the radical potential of bodies moving together in space.

The three of us wrote "The Deep" together. (Since each of us was several, there was already quite a crowd.) We did so at the request of *This American Life* producers Stephanie Foo, Neil Drumming, and Ira Glass, who commissioned the song for their episode "We Are in the Future" and each gave generous notes contributing to the final result. We emphasize collaborative authorship at every stage of this ongoing work because collaboration and collectivity tie into our initial idea for the song. The first rule we established shortly after clipping. formed was that Daveed's lyrics should never be written from a first-person perspective—this extended to the banishment of all first-person pronouns and possessives: *I, me, my,* etc. For "The Deep," we continued to follow this rule, but narrowed it even further: the only pronoun allowed in the song was *y'all*. Our prohibition of the first person was, in part, a reaction to the fiercely individualistic authorship presumed in rap lyrics, so in imagining what a Drexciyan utopia might look like, through the lens of clipping.'s linguistic rules, we imagined their culture might affirm collectivity over the individual, and therefore, the plural over the singular. The word *y'all*, for us, became both an emblem of the Drexciyans' advanced communal society, and a reference to the multiple-authorship of the song, shared between those of us in clipping. and our partners at *This American Life*, as well as with Drexciya and their collaborators.

Now, Rivers has contributed their misheard whisper to the chain, filling out our song's narrative with their particular concerns, politics, infatuations, and passions. Rivers has fixed on the refrain *Y'all remember*, which is repeated many times throughout our song. They have expanded that phrase into a major aspect of their world-building. In our song, the lyrics serve as a kind of ceremonial performance of remembering. We conceived it as something like a Passover Seder, where the history of whatever new society is formed after the Drexciyans rise up against the surface world is retold. Now we've learned who is burdened with this ritual of remembering and retelling. Rivers has given us Yetu, and in so doing, shown us something that our song elided: the immediate and visceral pain inherent in passing down past trauma. Drexciya's militant uprising, which we suggested was incited by climate change and the destruction of Earth's oceans, becomes an ambivalent act of both justice and extreme violence, perpetuating further trauma. In their translation from Drexciya to clipping. to this book, Rivers has added a dimension of pain to all three texts.

Yetu's painful remembering might be seen as an allegory for the painful process of adaptation that Rivers has accomplished by retelling a fictional, but nonetheless consequential, story of white supremacist violence. It's a retelling that reaches back to the materials it adapts, and complicates them; makes them better. In this sense, Rivers has coauthored our song in as profound a way as we have inspired this book.

Ever since the book's announcement, we've been asked by fans and journalists if Rivers's version of the story is "canon." The answer is yes, and no. Part of our rejection of first-person perspective is also a rejection of the authoritative position that the notion of a canon assumes. Readers and listeners have before them three—let's call them objects of study: the recorded oeuvre of Drexciya and its associated artwork and liner notes, the clipping. song "The Deep," and Rivers Solomon's novella *The Deep*. We prefer to imagine each of these objects as artifacts—as primary sources—each showing a different angle on a world whose nature can never be observed in totality. Each contributor has told their story about the same underwater city, and each telling has its own specific perspective, the way any two "true stories" about our own world can provide differing, or even incompatible, visions of our reality. Experiencing these works requires labor—something like that of an archaeologist who's discovered multiple texts about the Drexciyan civilization and is tasked with assembling a picture of that civilization. We ask a lot of our readers and listeners. This is why we will return to the metaphor of the game of Telephone—it's no fun with one person, and the joy of it is that no misheard utterance is more "correct" or "true" than any other. The pleasure is in the process, and the value is not in any one version of the phrase but in its gradual transformation purple monkey dishwasher

ACKNOWLEDGMENTS

I AM THANKFUL FOR THE OCEAN, FROM WHICH LIFE springs. I am thankful for the ancestors, who lived, which is all any of us can do. And I am thankful for our vast human history, wide and various enough that there are legacies of triumph for every legacy of trauma. Everything is always changing, which means nothing can ever be hopeless. The battering rush of tides shapes and smooths rock, carves out new lands.

I am one person in a great network of people who made *The Deep* possible. It could not have happened without Navah, who dreamed up this seed and trusted me with its nurturing. All books are collaborative efforts, but this book more than average. Without the permission and support of clipping. to use their profoundly powerful sound "The Deep," this text would not exist.

Thank you to my agent Laura, who always has my

interests at heart, who calms my anxieties, who roots for me. Thank you to my partner, who is an editor, a support group, and a damn fine human all in one. To Bunny, who is my dearest friend and keeps me alive. To my mother, who is always there. To my grandmother, who is no longer here, but who is still always there. To Johnny, Susannah, Ibrahim, Johanna, Alice, and Aaron at Akashic Books, who published my very first book, who took an incredible leap of faith on me, without whom this second book would not exist.

—Rivers Solomon

THE

DEEP

RIVERS SOLOMON

THIS READING GROUP GUIDE FOR *THE DEEP* INCLUDES an introduction, discussion questions, and ideas for enhancing your book club. The suggested questions are intended to help your reading group find new and interesting angles and topics for your discussion. We hope that these ideas will enrich your conversation and increase your enjoyment of the book.

Introduction

Yetu holds the memories for her people—water-dwelling descendants of pregnant African slave women thrown overboard by slave owners—who live idyllic lives in the deep. Their past, too painful to be remembered regularly, is forgotten by everyone, save one: the historian. This demanding role has been bestowed on Yetu. Yetu remembers for everyone, and the memories, harrowing and wonderful, traumatic and terrible, are destroying her. And so, she flees to the surface, escaping the memories, the expectations, and the responsibilities—and discovers a world her people left behind long ago. Yetu will learn more than she ever expected to about her own past—and about the future of her people. If they are all to survive, they'll need to reclaim the memories, reclaim their identity—and own who they really are.

Topics & Questions for Discussion

1. We meet Yetu, the historian, at a vulnerable moment in her life when all her pain is on display. Describe her character and emotional state as it is revealed during this raw introduction.

2. As the historian, Yetu faces death and suffering daily while the other wajinru live free from the burdens of the past. How does Yetu's understanding of pain and grief further separate her from her people? Discuss how the rememberings have shaped Yetu and why her kin cannot understand.

3. The rememberings appear to bring Yetu both pain and comfort. What about these memories bring Yetu peace? Why does she often choose them over life in the present?

4. In chapter 3 the origins of the wajinru are revealed. Discuss the intertwining of mankind's history with theirs. How does the violence in the foremothers' lives and deaths influence the way the wajinru live? Why is it crucial that the historian remember but the rest of the people forget this piece of their history?

5. Discuss Yetu's decision to flee from her people, a choice that means abandoning her family, the History and the only way of life she's ever known. Think of a comparable situation in our world. What would you have done in her position? Should she have handled the situation differently or are her actions justified?

6. The first historian, Zoti, had pure intentions when they began the rememberings cycle, "I fear if they know the truth of everything, they will not be able to carry on, or they'll swim to the surface to learn things for themselves I do not want them to learn." (page 63) How justified is it for Zoti to make this decision for the whole species? Does it help or hinder the growth of their community? Provide examples.

7. As the reader we are privy to select moments from the History. Why is Zoti's experience meeting Waj one of them? What does it reveal? Why is it significant to Zoti individually and the wajinru people as a whole?

8. Yetu longed for the ignorant bliss of the other wajinru but the experience is different than she imagined: "The emptiness inside her stretched far and wide in every direction like a cavern. It was lonely. She had thought herself unmoored when she was the historian, but this did not compare. She was a blip." (page 78) Discuss the emptiness she describes and what it must be like to lose that piece of herself. Is happiness possible for Yetu?

9. Yetu does not pretend to have forgotten her people or the pain she knows they are experiencing. How does she rationalize her decision to leave and her plan to stay away? What drove her to this point and did she have other options?

10. When Yetu is beached, she has nothing but faint recollections of the two-legs to guide her, and her relationship with Oori becomes very important to her. Why are their interactions so significant? What valuable lessons does Oori teach Yetu?

11. In flashbacks we see that life as a new historian was exceptionally difficult for Yetu, and they hint at the road she eventually takes. Describe her Amaba's behavior during this time. Is she unable to understand Yetu's pain, or is it a choice? What do these flashbacks reveal about those who live free of the History?

12. Chapter 8 is told from the perspective of a former historian, Basha. His experience of the rememberings is the polar opposite of Yetu's. Discuss how these two historians differ and why. Are there any parallels between their lives? What does a glimpse into his time as the historian reveal?

13. The choice to return home is not an easy one for Yetu, but in Chapter 9 she is finally driven to do so. What was the catalyst that pushed her past her fear? How has

her understanding of her responsibilities changed when she returns home? Why might this new mind-set be critical for her and the wajinru's survival?

14. Sharing the burden of the rememberings with all wajinru turns out to be the healthiest outcome for everyone. Not only are the people more whole for it, but Yetu can finally find some peace. Discuss the other pros and cons of this new way of life and how it will impact the wajinru going forward.

Enhance Your Book Club

1. This story juxtaposes life with and without access to and an understanding of history. Discuss how people and societies are hindered when they disregard the past. Examine the importance of teaching people their history and the dangers of hiding any aspect of it.

2. Imagine you are one of the wajinru. Would you rather be a historian like Yetu or one of the blissfully ignorant wajinru? Share why you would choose one existence over the other. How might this existence differ from the way you engage with history now?

3. The mythos of *The Deep* was born from one of the darkest pieces of mankind's history. Read the afterword and discuss the scope of the narrative Rivers Solomon created. Why was it important to put things in this context? What does it reveal about the way people in the twenty-first century deal with the past? Are we so different from the wajinru?